JUST A PAINTER

A DAVID AND TRAIT MYSTERY

SHANE CHASTAIN

3MG BOOKS

CHAPTER ONE

JUST A PAINTER

"Well, you've done it now, Dave," I said, shaking my head in disgust.

"It's fine, John."

"Cut it out!" He hit the starter for the second time, causing a sharp ejection of white smoke to escape through the open dipstick hole.

"It's not fine, Dave. I asked you about the oil. I always ask you about the oil. How many times, this week, have I asked you about the oil?"

Dave leaned out from the driver's side window and tried to defend himself.

"You ask me about the gas and oil." He said it like he was reminding me of something important.

I tried to stay calm and explained.

"David DeGrabber, your car is a damn 32'. It goes through oil at nearly the same rate as gas. You ran it out, and now it's toast." I stuck the bone dry dipstick back into the motor and closed the hood. "It'll need a rebuild, at best, and probably a new motor."

Dave got out and closed his door. He looked into the old blue sedan with a sour expression. Now he crossed his arms and turned to me, looking toward the ground, his ever shaggy dark hair obscuring his eyes. He spoke.

"We'll have to call a wrecker."

"We will."

He looked up and down the empty, early dawn street. I made a suggestion.

"We might as well keep going into town until we find a booth, or a drugstore that's already open."

He raised the shoulders of his navy blue jacket and let them fall. We started down the sidewalk.

To the David and Trait Detective Agency, of which Dave and I are the whole, the loss of our fleet would not be understated as dire. It was Dave's sedan, and unless he had some money put away, and I mean put all the way away, we were in for hardship. The entirety of my emergency fund would have scarcely replaced a flat on our company car, much less pay for a new motor.

I was good and sore at Dave for a number of reasons. Walking down the street in the early dawn light, or mostly darkness, as it was, I can't be bothered to order them by anything.

First, we had gone over to Michigan for a private investigator's conference, where they had asked Dave to give a talk. It had been a paying gig, but Dave had bungled the arrangement with the rooms, and so we were caught out on Sunday night. It was either, pay a premium that would have put us upside down for the trip, or head back in the dark. We'd decided to go home. Dave said he felt good to drive, so somewhere around Kalamazoo, I fell asleep. I don't know if it was the cool late summer air that did it, or the energy used in handing out cards and giving sales pitches, but I had managed to sleep through the motor's death rattles.

That makes me mad, and brings me to the second point. David DeGrabber is brilliant. I'm no slouch myself, believe you me, but Dave can do things that normal people can't. He can remember everything. He can work out any set of figures, instantly. He can put seemingly unrelated things together, as though he kept them right at hand. When he's interested. That's the problem, too. Cars don't interest Dave. To him they may as well be dogs or horses. If they were dogs or horses, maybe they'd walk up to him and find a way to let him know they're hungry. Long ago, I'd given up on keeping track of times that Dave had ran his car out of gas, and have taken it upon myself to handle most of the maintenance. I thought, surely my hounding about the fluids would be enough for something so simple, but apparently not. It's a wonder we had even made it back into Chicago. The old blue sedan had given it up on some side street, just on the south side. Dave had taken it off of the main thoroughfares as the engine lost power, and could no longer maintain highway speeds. I had half a mind to ask him what he thought when that started, but decided his answer might enrage me, so I just kept trudging.

The side streets of the south side were not scenic, so it

didn't hurt my feelings that the sights were mostly still concealed behind the last moments of night.

"What do you suppose any of this means, John?" Dave asked thoughtfully.

I didn't hear his steps behind, so I stopped and turned to see what he was talking about. We were beneath a small two-lane overpass. He had stopped halfway and was inspecting the block wall. I recovered the twenty feet that separated us and took a look. It was hard to make out, as there was hardly any light under the overpass to speak of.

"Maybe an angel, or a bull?" I offered. "Something with points, or limbs, coming off the sides," I pointed out.

"Maybe so. Done in spray paint, I think."

I stood for another two seconds, with no comment, before I turned and resumed my march. Sure, I thought, white spray paint on concrete block. If the world ends tomorrow, maybe some future species will break the chunk of wall out and stick it in a museum, as some kind of ancient artistic wonder. That's the sort of outlandishness it would have to be for that sorry bull-angel piece of vandalism to be anything more than a waste of paint, time, and wall.

Emerging from the depression that made up the underpass, I spotted salvation at the corner. A filling station, with a payphone outside. I picked up my step, got to the receiver, and dialed the operator. I told her to get me a wrecker, and craned my neck to see the street sign, to tell where to send it. With the truck on its way, and it being Monday morning, if only just, I dialed Sid, our building doorman, at his house. He picked up groggy.

"Hello, who's this?"

"Sid, it's John."

"Who?"

"John Trait." I flicked my arm around for my watch. "Sid, you get ready for work in an hour. Clear the webs out, will ya?"

I think I heard him shudder all over. Now, somewhat clearer headed, he spoke.

"Sorry, what's going on, John?" he smacked.

"Dave ran the car out of oil, and we're stranded. The tow truck is on the way, but we may be late getting into the office today. If we get any early callers, you try to hold them till we get there. This thing with the car is gonna be expensive, so we can't miss anybody."

"Sure thing. No problem. Good luck with the truck."

He hung up.

His affirmative didn't fill me with a whole lot of confidence, but I wasn't wasting another dime on it. I put the receiver back on the hook and checked the coin return. Empty. We started back to the car to wait.

Tow truck drivers never hurry. On a call for a breakdown, they have a captive clientele. Dave and I sat in the sedan, which smelled of burnt piston rings, until the sun was well up above the houses. That was the scenery, by the way. Short houses, with unkept yards. When the wrecker finally did show, the driver looked well rested, and ready to tackle his day. He was a rotund fellow, with a mustache, and had a hearty laugh when I told him why we shouldn't bother trying to start it again. He got the car loaded in no time, and we rode three abreast to a shop that my friend Carl owns.

Carl had a laugh too, while we dropped the car off. It was nearly ten, and I couldn't even look at Dave. He didn't seem ashamed at all. He kept telling people how it broke down, as if it was some sort of regular occurrence. He even had the audacity to ask Carl how soon he could have it back. Carl looked to me incredulously. I didn't blame him, and shuffled Dave out of the shop and down the street to catch the L train to the office.

With the morning as good as spent, our finances suddenly in peril, and without shaves or showers, we finally arrived at the four story square building, at the edge of downtown, that holds our office and not much else.

"Did you get the car fixed?" It was Sid, from behind his desk. He was having an early lunch, and sat reclined in his chair, with a sack of something perched on his ample belly.

I just shrugged and went for the stairs. We have an elevator, but I didn't feel like I deserved to bother Sid about it. Something about a night's sleep in a car puts me on the wrong foot. I drug myself up with the rail, but heard how Dave had taken the elevator. He must have had a word with Sid, because I emerged from the stairwell as he did the elevator.

"We have a client waiting," he announced, adjusting his jacket collar.

"Sid has a key?" I asked, turning the knob at our office door.

"I left mine with him, in case he needed anything while we were gone."

I told my head to shake a little, but it might not have bothered to. I held the door and let Dave lead the way.

Our client had sat herself, or maybe Sid had sat her, right at the ends of our cheap matching desks, that faced each other, near the far wall. Our office wasn't much. From the back wall it went, file cabinet with radio, then two desks and chairs, sat at right angles to the door. Beyond them we'd added a red rug. We had two little safes too, on each side. Walls, white. Couple of floor lamps. One oil painting by Dave's grandmother.

The woman stood and turned to face us as we entered. Dave must have got a name downstairs.

"Hello, Miss Scudder. You may keep your seat." We made our way around to our desk chairs, and shook her hand as we sat. "My name is David DeGrabber, and this is my colleague, John Trait. How may we help you?"

CHAPTER TWO

———————

Sally Scudder, our guest, stood around five seven, in white shoes with the smallest of heel. She wore a sky blue dress with a tan belt around the middle. Her figure was fair, but not anything special. She looked early twenties, and her cheeks were a noticeable amount broader than her temples, but she fixed her blonde hair in a way to compensate.

After standing for introductions, she sat back down and started with her problem.

"I found your agency in the paper a while back. I've been looking for something, like you all, since a couple of weeks after it happened. I just feel like nobody cares, you know. I phoned the other agencies in town, but they acted like they weren't any more interested than the police have been."

Dave held a hand up for her to yield. I'm glad he did, because I was about to.

"Miss Scudder," he began delicately. "I think you may

be excited about your visit today, and may have started your tale some place other than the beginning." She opened her mouth, as if to say, "Oh," and closed it again. "Tell us what thing has befallen you, please," Dave concluded.

Sally Scudder intertwined her fingers and brought them up near her chin with a deep breath and lowered them again. She started more cohesively this time.

"My father, Roy Scudder, was found dead last month. Murdered."

There was something for the old notepad. I shifted in my chair to a more attentive position. Dave put his pad on his desk and crossed his arms for murder thinking. She went on.

"The police came and looked the place over. They talked to me and some of our acquaintances, but didn't seem to make much headway, and then, after a week, just stopped trying."

"What did your father-" Dave and I had questioned simultaneously. I closed my trap and gave an eye to Dave to go ahead. He did.

"What did you father do, Miss Scudder?"

Telling of the thing didn't seem to be hurting her, so she answered straight.

"He was just a painter. You can call me Sally."

Dave's a stickler for some things.

"And what were the circumstances of your father's death, Miss Scudder?"

She raised her bundled hands up from her lap and let them drop a second time.

It looks like someone came into his garage, where he keeps his supplies, and stabbed him to death. He has, or I guess had, a helper, and he found him there that morning. The police say he had been killed some time around midnight, the night before."

"The helper's name?" Dave asked.

"His name is Dick Templeton. The police talked to him, and I have too. He was just a young man my dad hired to carry paint, really. He seemed upset for having seen the body."

I had a leading comment and made it.

"So, Sally, I guess you want us to try to track down your father's killer, and you think we might have more luck than the police?"

"I do," she plainly stated. "Well, I hope you do. I just think, since he wasn't anyone special, that they didn't think it was worth much time. You've seen the papers, those stories about the missing debutantes? They're getting all the attention. Not some old drunk painter."

She had slid that drunk tag in there, not with vitriol or shame, but with a hint of a smile. I got the impression that she and her dad had been close. It added a level to the thing, as well.

"Your father drank, Miss Scudder?" Dave asked.

She flipped it away with a hand.

"He did," she admitted. "But he went to work, and usually did a good job. He was a good man, Mr. DeGrabber. Don't think he wasn't. He did wonderfully by me, and got me grown up, and into college. I graduate next year from Loyola." She beamed on that last part.

"Do you know of anybody that your pop might have had a problem with, or someone that might have had a problem with him?" I asked.

"Well, there's my mother, and his second wife. They weren't exactly fans of his, but I don't think for a second they would have wanted to kill him."

I asked for names all the same, and took them down.

"Anybody else? Bad business, irate clients, maybe somebody outside a liquor store?" I tried to keep it casual. She thought for a second and answered sheepishly.

"Well, he did get into a fight with Ellen's new boyfriend."

I had Ellen Scudder down in my notes as the most recent ex wife.

Dave jumped on it.

"Tell us about that, please."

She swung over to Dave and gave it to us like a news report.

"My father got drunk, three days before his murder. He missed work that day, and decided to drop in on Ellen. She had found another boyfriend. Ed Wallace, nicknamed Wally, who's not only my age, but is also enrolled at the college. I wouldn't know anything about Ellen if it weren't for her hunting within my peer group. Anyway, my dad liked her, and sometimes still did. Around five o'clock, he pulled up in his truck, took out a planter with his bumper, and started professing his love there in the yard. Wally came out, and they shoved around. My dad hit him and blacked his eye, before Ellen threatened to call the police." She sighed. "I only know all this because it went around campus. Wally spun it that he had won the fight, of course, but he told what really happened to a couple of girls, and they gossiped. I asked dad about it, but he said he couldn't remember, and I'm sure that was true."

"You gave all that to the police, I hope?" said Dave.

She shook her head.

"I did. Ellen called me, saying they had brought Wally in for questioning after the murder. She seemed to think I had inconvenienced them. I told her where she could stick it."

I tilted my head in quiet admiration. Sally Scudder was growing on me.

"Well, they must have let him go, or you wouldn't be here. Any idea what he had for an alibi?" I asked.

She shook her head that she didn't and said as much.

"The last update I managed to get out of the police, was that they were, 'Looking at other suspects." She put the quotes around that with her fingers.

I looked over to Dave. He was staring down, arms still crossed, in the vicinity of Sally's footwear. Receiving no opinion, I began handling the business of getting things underway.

"We can look into this for you, Sally. I need to warn you that this kind of thing can be expensive."

I let it sit like that, having delivered it with all the delicacy and reverence I had learned to muster over the years. She just blinked at me, as though she expected me to continue. After a brief moment, she spoke.

"Money isn't much of a concern for me anymore, Mr. Trait."

"Well, that's just wonderful," I exclaimed with a smile.

Dave wasn't as exuberant.

"Did your father leave you a large inheritance, Miss Scudder? I don't mean to be invasive, but the transfer of sums might motivate auxiliary parties in all manner of ways."

She held a palm out to the ground, toward Dave. Maybe she thought he needed soothing.

"It's fine, Mr. DeGrabber, really. I understand you all need to know everything you can to help. The police certainly did. It's a funny story, actually. My father drank, as you know, and a short time after I was born, he got the idea to add gambling to his list of hobbies. My mother threw a fit, of course, but he went to the track, anyway. You won't believe what happened."

We sat for an awkward pause until I thought to make a gesture with my face that said I would try to believe it.

"He won every race. It was just dumb luck, but he had snuck out with our entire life's savings. Then he did the most shocking thing of all." I thought we'd have another pause, so I got the face ready again, but she went right on this time. "He put it all back for his retirement. I asked him why he hadn't gone back to the track to try to win some more, and he told me that he didn't think he'd ever get that lucky again. He was probably right too."

"Now, I bet you're thinking, 'How did he keep it through the divorce?' right? Well, when things started to go sour with my mother, he let a friend of his invest it all, in different ways, to make it hard for her to get at, and it's been maturing ever since. Between that, and his life insurance, I was left a little over $50,000."

She beamed some more. Now, fifty grand is a lot more money than I have, but it is well within the realm of my imagination, and with the ever rising cost of everything, I felt like she oversold her windfall. Then again, maybe she was just happy to have something to remember her father by, and he didn't sound like he had come by money in many dependable ways. It was nothing to sneeze at either, for a twenty something college student.

Dave had either skipped his share of considering on the point, or had done so very fast, because he was right behind her again with another question.

"You are the sole heir, Miss Scudder?"

"I am," she stated, with a quick nod.

"Is your father's house still as it was when he was killed?" Dave asked dryly.

Another nod.

"Very well, Miss Scudder. John and I can begin on your case immediately. We will need a retainer, however. Two hundred dollars should do."

She nodded again, and reached for a bag she had at her feet. From it she drew a lady's wallet, unclasped it, and pulled a stack of cash out. It was a big stack. I tried not to gawk, but I wanted to ask if she had the whole fifty G's on her person. She fumbled some bills into her lap, but didn't let any reach the floor. She apologized a few times, as she wrestled the bag, the wallet, and the handful of money. Finally, she got two hundred arranged, and passed it over to Dave. He received it with his most gracious smile. I got a book of receipt carbons from my desk and filled out a slip, while Dave made a second count.

"Thank you for coming, Miss Scudder," Dave said, holding a hand out for a shake. He put the bills, counted and stacked, on the corner of his desk. "We'll get started right away. John, you have a list ready to add addresses to?"

"Yes, sir." I passed the receipt over. "Here you are, Sally. For your records."

She thanked me, and stuffed the slip, loose, into the recesses of the bag. I collected addresses and phone numbers to go with the names in my notes, and saw her out the door.

With goodbyes said, I closed the office door behind her, and made my way back to my desk. Standing on the rug, I looked over my notes again. The residence of the late Roy Scudder was an address in West Town, by the park. Dave had heard the address anyway, so I only shared my comments on it.

"Her old man's house isn't worlds away, but it'll be dark by the time we get there if we walk."

Dave was working through the bills again, and held out what looked like half. I thumbed through and confirmed I had a hundred.

"Split a cab?" I offered.

He sat for a second, and then sprung to his feet. It looked to me that his mood had soured, like mine, but with some money, and something to do, I didn't see why.

"Let's go down for lunch first," he stated, walking by me toward the door.

I caught the sound of a growl emanating from his

stomach as he passed. That's why his mood had turned. Dave is by no means a big man, but whereas I maintain the fighting shape of my army days, Dave tries to keep the thinnest layer of insulation on his frame at all times. Between that and his longer than average legs, his profile never screams athletic, but I had seen him execute some impressive feats.

I went in my desk for a fresh pencil, tucked it into my jacket pocket, and hurried out the door. With Dave's mood like it was, I didn't trust him to hold the elevator, and I had gotten too hungry for stairs myself.

CHAPTER THREE

Lunch was done on a budget. Though we had some money in our pockets, there was no guarantee there was any more coming behind it. It is often the opinion of outsiders, that us private dicks think low of the city's official investigators, and that's just not true. They do a fine job at most things, and considering the scale of their operation, I figure it's as good as can possibly be done. It's that scale, however, that creates the fringes and corners for Dave and I, and guys like us, to fill in. They just have too much to do, and more every day, whereas Dave and I had this one job. All that said, we ate bologna sandwiches from the corner haberdashery, because Sally Scudder might be wrong, and the police may have squeezed all there was to get out of her father's murder.

Our cab dropped us off in front of a single story white house, a block north of Humboldt Park, on the western edge of West Town. It wasn't anything special. The telltale signs of an occupant that probably shouldn't have been driving were there, but I might have missed them without the foreknowledge of them. The mailbox, with Scudder on its side, was dented and wobbled on its post. Looking down the side drive, toward the garage, I spied a salmon colored pickup with evidence of minor impacts on its driver's side mirror.

We started toward the garage right away, but were stopped by a man on the other side of a chest high fence.

"You two looking for something?" the man asked. He was ostensibly picking around on a hedge on his side of the fence, but I hadn't noticed him as we pulled up, so I think he had just hurried to the spot while we payed the cabbie. Dave gave him an answer plainly enough.

"Mr. Scudder's daughter has hired my colleague and I to look into her father's passing."

"Oh, yeah?" he said suspiciously. He tilted his head back as though he was really studying Dave. I shook my head at him. He had all the hallmarks of a nosey neighbor. Some forty-five years old, unimpressive build, glasses, and hair that needed combed.

"So, you're a couple of those P.I.'s, are you? I don't suppose you've got any licenses you can show me, do you?"

Dave reached into his pocket for his wallet, with no argument, but maybe my mood hadn't improved as much after lunch as I had hoped, so I made one.

"You're really about your P's and q's with the check-ins here, comrade. I don't suppose you happened to ask the guy that croaked Roy Scudder for his papers, did you?"

Dave had already handed him a document card, and

he was looking it over, holding his glasses over the top of his eyes. He turned a sour puss to me.

"The neighborhood is changing all the time, pal. You can never be too careful."

"And yet a guy gets offed, right next door, under your nose."

Dave used some words to referee.

"Did you happen to see, or hear, anything the night it happened? Mr.?"

"Thomas. Frank Thomas. No, I didn't see anything, because me and the wife had been out of town that weekend."

"What day did it happen?"

"Saturday, I think it was. Yeah, that's it. When we got back home, Sunday evening, they still had police around cleaning up and checking on things."

"Thank you, Mr. Thomas. I hope you have no objection to our being here," Dave said.

"Oh, no. If the daughter hired you, she hired you. It's none of my business."

I wasn't through with Frank Thomas.

"Where did you take the wife that weekend?" I asked.

"Lake Koshkonong," he answered. Looking like he'd had his fill of us now that questions had started his way, he abandoned his horticulture and went back to his house. Dave and I stood in the drive, and watched him till he was inside.

"That lake's about shallow enough to stand in," I commented.

Dave was looking into his breast pocket, getting his

things rearranged. He said, "Yes, it's not exactly a resort. We'll check his alibi if necessary."

We started down the drive.

"I'm not saying he did it. I think his hobbies are probably limited to butting in on whatever someone's doing outside his front window. Killing his next-door neighbor would be like canceling his own favorite program."

Dave didn't hear my joke, or maybe he wasn't paying attention. He went around the corner of the garage to retrieve a key, that Sally had told us about, from a gap in the window trim. The garage had a door on the right, along with the big flip up one. The key was suppose to fit the big door and did. Dave lifted it and revealed a surprise to me.

"Well, I had him pegged for the wrong kind of painter," I exclaimed.

"I did too. It seems Roy Scudder was indeed just a house painter."

I had expected easels, mixing boards, works in various stages of completion. Maybe even a smock, the original color uncertain, due to the abstract that years of little speckling and splatters had created on it. I expected there to be stacks of canvases. There were, in fact, stacks of canvas, in the form of a four by eight foot section of the garage that was dedicated to drop cloth storage. The middle of the room was littered with various buckets of paint, leftover from jobs, or bought and intended for future ones. On the left side of the room stood a row of thick fluffy rollers of various lengths and sizes, along with their poles. The back wall had a workbench that stretched nearly the width of the room. A sink had been installed for the cleaning of brushes, and many sat around the station.

Dave strolled around with his hands in his pockets, taking in the details as he came to them. He said nothing. I started making a lap as well. I had excepted us to get a look at the man, or at least who he had been, by the arrangement of his art studio. Had he been a simple and utilitarian sort, with a single easel and project, and the whole space dedicated to its creation, or was he the avant garde type, with candles, and other works hung around for inspiration? This house painter's storage shed, as it amounted to, didn't tell me much right off.

Dave made his way to the far corner from the door, where a sitting area had been arranged by the bench, next to a gas heater on the wall. He perched himself on the stool, and picked up a short glass from the bench top. He smelled of it.

"Scotch," he determined.

I watched as Dave got himself comfortable. He leaned into the bench top and played the glass around. Resting it on his leg for a moment, and moving it back to the other hand, and trying out different places for it on the bench top. He swiveled around, faced the wall, and went into his pocket for a cigarette, then stopped and put them back. I approached. The corner area had a lot of different things at hand, and Dave had found papers and tobacco with which to roll a smoke. He was doing that, and sitting low, as Roy Scudder might have after a day's work and an evening's drink. He spoke softly as he worked the paper around.

"Roy Scudder spent a great deal of time here."

"You think he just used the house for sleeping and cooking?"

"We'll get in and see for sure, but I think this is the spot." He leaned back, and directed me to a shelf by his knee. "Most of his things are here. What liquor he could keep at hand, some bottles with only tastes left, his tobacco. Hello, what have we here?"

Dave had lit his smoke with a lighter from the bench and had been studying it. Now his eye caught a worn notebook. He picked it up and passed it to me. It was just a cheap black book, with yellow colored lined pages. It was clearly a schedule and contacts book. The whole thing was one entry after another, of a client's name, address, and number, and below that, a note of the paint color, and what the paint was supposed to go on. Finally, a dollar figure concluded each entry, with a check mark next to it, presumably indicating a balance received. I shared with Dave.

"It's a list of his jobs. No dates, though." I passed it back. Dave puffed on his smoke as he flipped through the pages.

"Hmm. We must assume it to be sequential, of course. I count three different pencils, at least, by the weight of the lines, and two types of pen ink. This book accounts for a fair amount of the deceased's work history."

He leaned over and puffed some smoke into my face as he pointed to a page.

"Look here, toward the end. There are four pages of entries under this heading, with only an unpaid painting of a living room during that time."

"C.P.D." I read. "The police department?"

"The Park District, I think, more likely. Many of these entries have no location, just the price, but the ones that do are bathrooms, benches, and the odd office."

"There are a couple, at the end that he doesn't have marked paid. We should go to the parks office, and see if he had any trouble on some of these jobs." I noted an entry, and said, "I wonder what happened with Mrs. Washington's living room, too? It comes in at the top of page two of the city stuff, and he's paid all the way through to the last three of the fourth page, so he had time to get it done."

I'd taken the book back, and Dave was checking through another stack of documents. The one in his hand now, he felt, was worth mentioning.

"I believe I have your answer, John."

He handed me a short letter. Typed.

Mr. Scudder, my wife and I are contacting you, certified, to inform you of our intent to pursue whatever legal recourse we may have against you. The state of our kitchen, living room, and entryway is unacceptable. The damages to the floor alone have been quoted to us at no less than $2,000.00. The damage to our belongings is much more. The finish of the piano, being an antique, is virtually irreparable. We cannot fathom what came over you, but do intend for you to pay.

Fred Washington

. . .

I gave a low whistle.

"Sounds like Scudder had a bad day at the office." I looked back at the notebook. "He was only set to make $250 on the job."

"Yes, we'll need to speak with the Washington's. It seems unlikely they would resort to murder, having expressed litigiousness, but possibly the loss of something they felt irreplaceable drove them to more aggressive actions."

I handed the notebook and letter back to Dave, and he put them in his pockets. I made an observation.

"They might have got disheartened about their suit, when they thought about what good it'd be to go after a drunk house painter. Sally didn't make it sound like Roy was the sort to flash his money around, or even keep it around."

"Let's look in the house," Dave said, sliding the stool back and getting to his feet. He crushed out the last of his smoke on a spot on the bench that had been used for it.

We made our way out slowly, trying to find anything else to jump out at us, but without any details on the attack, beyond it being a stabbing, or the position of the body, we couldn't know if Roy Scudder had been cut down answering the door, sitting at his bench, or checking the garage for a strange noise in the middle of the night. Dave pulled the garage door back down, locked it, and returned the key to its hiding place.

I looked over the pickup. I don't mean to besmirch Roy

Scudder, or his trade. I certainly don't hold some opinion, or assume that tradesmen have some predisposition for moral ineptitude. Quite the contrary. My pop was a cabinet man and still is. Looking at Roy Scudder's truck though, the evidence was too strong to ignore. He had a monkey on his back, and wasn't trying especially hard to shake it off. The front bumper made the mailbox and side mirrors look factory fresh. Not hanging off, or totally smashed in, but dinged, like the brakes just couldn't quite catch right all the time. The passenger floor board showed what was slowing them down, as it was full of beer cans, of all cheap varieties. The pile was nearly level with the seat.

"John," Dave called to me, bringing me from my considerations. He was up four steps, on a landing outside the back door of the house. I climbed the stairs as he jiggled the knob.

"Here," he offered. "I'll stand and obstruct Mr. Thomas' view, while you pick the lock."

Dave handed me a small pouch, containing the necessary equipment. I glanced over both shoulders to make sure I didn't have an audience, bent down, and got to work.

Residential doorknob. Non-emergency. Daylight. Time to open: thirty seconds.

With the job done, beside a most casual looking Dave, I pushed the door open and we went inside. I handed Dave back his things as I looked around.

The back door put us in a dusty kitchen. Dishes and glasses were still in the sink, looking as though they'd already had a long wait for a wash. Further into the home, the little signs of someone with a problem, from outside,

25

were more pronounced within. It was a shrine, in a way, to a happier time. The decor clearly had a woman's touch, but it was also plain that it had not been touched in some time. A layer of dust rested on all the tables, mirrors, and accessories. A television set sat on a hutch in the main room, across from a beige couch that was beginning to look threadbare in places.

"He slept here on the couch," I observed. The two sleeping pillows, stacked on one end, and looking like they had been half sat on, clued me in. Dave grunted that he heard me, and went down a hall to the rest of the rooms.

I thought I might try Dave's method, and so plopped down in what would have been Roy Scudder's spot, and tried to get into character. I might as well have poured myself a drink, or three, since there was no danger of needing to drive anywhere. I hopped up, and reached over a cluttered coffee table, and turned the set on. As I fell back down into the couch, as Scudder surely had, my hand fell between the arm and cushion and onto something hard. I reached and pulled. What I got was a Luger pistol. I knew them well from finding them on German soldiers in the war. I popped the magazine out, inspected it, found it full, cleared the chamber, and sat that round on the table. The tv was on and playing some ads. I felt further down between the cushions on both sides, and found nothing but disconcerting feeling crumbs. I made a note to wash my hands.

"What are you doing?" Dave asked. He'd returned from his exploration, and stood behind me and the couch. I hopped up.

"Trying to get a feel for our stiff," I said. I held the pistol out for Dave to see, and added, "He should have had this with him."

Dave raised his eyebrows. "Indeed." He turned on his heel and started for the exit. I followed, and he spoke. "I'm going to check Roy Scudder's city jobs. I would like you to look at the ex wives, the boyfriend, Wally, the Washington's, and Templeton, the helper."

He had his hand on the back doorknob, and looked ready to bid me farewell. He'd already forgotten.

"We need to use the phone here to call another cab or two," I stated plainly.

"Yes." His shoulders dropped. "I suppose we do."

"I'll handle it. Sit tight." I turned and went through to the front of the house, turning the tv off as I passed. The phone hung on the wall, on the side of an opening to the entryway from the front room. I dialed the cab depot and asked for Ralph.

"Ralph, here," he announced.

"Hey, Ralph. John Trait. Yeah, work's going peachy. Listen, Dave and I are on foot. Can we get a couple cars out this way? I want one of them to be you. I'll tell you all about it. We'll have time."

I'll save you the rest of it. I gave the address to Ralph, and he promised to be by soon. I hung up and put my hand to my face, thinking if there was anybody else I needed to call while it didn't cost me anything. The stubble I felt added another errand to my list. I dialed the garage, where we'd dropped the car off, and asked how late Carl planned to be there. He said he was plenty busy, and would stay till well after dinnertime. I told him to expect me. The reason was that our suitcases were still in the trunk, and I can't speak for Dave, but I only had the one shaving set. For the sake of being thorough, I called at the office and asked Sid if we'd had any callers. He said no.

Dave had taken up after me, and so after Scudder, in sitting low on the end of the worn out couch. I reported my communiques, in case he hadn't heard, and plopped down at the other end to wait. It wasn't a bad couch. I yawned once, and then stifled the second, for fear that I might go out. I don't know how Dave resisted it after driving all night. After twenty minutes, we made our way back out onto the drive, locking ourselves out again, and waited another five before the cabs pulled up. During the wait, I copied my share of the black notebook, which was just the Washington's home address.

Ralph hadn't had nearly the strenuous weekend as Dave and I. He pulled up to the curb, and beckoned to me excitedly. Dave's man was someone I hadn't seen before. I got in, gave Ralph the address to the Washington's residence, and we pulled away.

CHAPTER FOUR

"Where's that old sedan? Your partner there usually don't need a driver." Ralph was nearly shouting. He always nearly shouted. He was a transplant from Boston, about sixty, and always happy. Today his voice pierced my head, even in the back seat, but he's the most dependable cabbie I know, and I already had him trained in tailing, waiting, and discrete pickups.

"Dave ran the sedan out of oil and blew it up on the way back from Detroit last night," I answered. It made me surly to say it out loud again, so I jumped at the chance to pile on Dave, when Ralph responded,

"What is he, a dope? How'd he not notice? I had a head gasket go bad once in a cab. It made an awful racket. He couldn't have missed it."

"You know, Ralph, he is a dope. I nag him like a wife, no less than three times a week, to make sure to keep some gas and oil in the damn thing, and he had the gall to act like I meant gas or oil."

"He's a putz, John. You should work for yourself. I always say, you should work for yourself. Don't I always say that?"

"I don't know about all that, but that's the part that gets me. He's not dumb. Just earlier he flips through a notebook and determines the guy's had it a while by being able to see how many pencils he'd gone through."

"How can he not read a dipstick?" Ralph tacked on.

"Exactly," I seethed.

"Here's the spot. You want me to wait?"

"Yes, sir," I said, climbing from the cab.

During my venting, Ralph had guided the car, in the efficient way that cabbies do, to a sprawling house that could have used a little more lot under it. The Washington's lived just off Lakeshore, in the EdgeWater district, where nothing was cheap or ugly. Ralph pulled right up to the front door, at the top of the circle drive. I got out and climbed the six steps to the door and worked the knocker. A man opened up that looked more the letter taking type, than the letter writing type. He was very formal and asked for a card. I gave him one, and he looked down his nose at it; not that he thought low of it, but more that it was part of the gig. He told me to wait, and closed up again. After no more than a minute, he returned and greeted me warmly. Not that he thought so high of me, but more that it was also part of the gig.

The sprawl on the inside made it so you could forgive there only being a few lawn mower passes of grass in the yard. The floors were dark oak, the walls paneled, the place smelled of fresh flowers, and there were paintings hung around. They'd even decided the wood floors might get boring, so they switched it up at intervals with rugs thick enough for a woman to lose an earring in.

The butler, as he may as well be called, led me through a main hall, and an auxiliary corridor, before holding open some double doors that went into a study.

"Mr. John Trait, to see you, sir," he announced.

With all that pomp and circumstance, you might expect there to have been a duke, or senator, or some kind of important person, within, and maybe Fred Washington was one or more of those things, but he didn't look it from where I stood.

"Oh, come in. Come in. Would you like a scotch, Mr. Trait?" my host asked.

"That'd be swell. Mr. Washington, I presume?"

He held out a hand for a shake, and put a glass in my other.

"Yeah. Yeah. Yeah. Call me Fred. Here, this is Steve Cecant. The next race is about to start. Do you gamble, Mr. Trait?"

Fred and Steve, both in shirtsleeves and brown slacks, with drinks in hand, were sitting right up close to a television set that had horse racing on it. It looked like it was a good time, and had been for some time. On a table, a ways back behind their heavy leather chairs, likely where they had started before moving up for a better view, sat a collection of trays and used glasses. The way it looked, they had run the butler ragged, and now had opted for the whole bottle. Fred was storing it on the floor next to the leg of the TV set. I stood between the chairs, sipped my drink, and watched them yell and cheer for their prospects for a quick three furloughs. Some money changed hands on the spot, with Steve the victor. The starting gun had saved me from having to get off on the bad foot of not having money enough to bet.

"Your card said you're a private detective, didn't it?" Fred asked.

"It did, indeed."

"You hired a detective, Fred? Are you gonna send him after that sorry painter?" That was Steve, with a knee slap.

"I might! Ha haha."

They were lit all the way up. I looked at my watch and read 2:37. Fred turned to me, marginally more serious, and asked, "How about that, Mr. Trait? I hired a painter awhile back, and he showed up drunk and destroyed some valuables, not to mention didn't paint the room. Do you handle that kind of thing?"

I answered friendly, so's not to sound like an agent of the enemy.

"That's actually why I'm here. I wanted to talk to you, and see what happened with all of that."

"He didn't hire you to come and move me off of the suit, I hope. You might as well hit the road, if that's it. My wife's never going to get over that painting he ruined, and she's not letting me off of it because I just tried to save a little money."

I showed him my palm, and took a big swig of my drink.

"No, sir. I'm not here about any suit. Roy Scudder's daughter hired me. Her father was murdered last month."

I let it sit like that, in case one of them started sweating bullets, or jumped and ran out the door. You know, something easy. As usual, they didn't do anything of the sort. It honestly didn't seem to dampen the mood all that much. They each took a big drink, and Fred reached for the bottle to refill. He spoke as he topped us all off.

"That's too bad. Roy was an all right guy. I went to school with him. I always thought he could have made something more of himself, if he'd just put that bottle down. Do they know who killed him?" Something occurred to him, and his tone hardened. "You surely don't think I had anything to do with it, do you?"

He looked half crazed, and half incredulous, but it was mainly the flush from the scotch. I put him back at ease.

"I'm not saying any of that, Mr. Washington. It's strictly routine to check around and talk with anybody that he might have had a problem with. We found the letter you sent him, you see."

He smirked with his brow furrowed in the middle, looking from me to his friend and back again. Finally, he offered,

"Well, you might as well ask your questions. Pull that chair up."

He pointed to a wooden dining chair along the wall. I went for it, and they slid around to make room. There wasn't much to it. By the time I left, two races and an hour and a half later, I had all there was to get by direct means.

Fred Washington ran a construction business, contracting the building of homes, like his, in the Lakeshore districts. Roy Scudder was the cheapest house painter in the city, and hadn't been working as much lately. Washington didn't know Roy had been painting for the city at the time. Anyhow, his wife wanted one of the living rooms, the one with the antique piano, painted maroon, in honor of their daughter's acceptance into Loyola University. The rest of the story went like you might imagine. Roy showed up bright and early, on an all night bender, and proceeded to forego drop cloths, or even the taking down of the paintings. He'd left a trail throughout the house from the service entrance of paint, dings in the floor, and chips in the paneling. The paint he brought hadn't even been maroon. Fred even showed me a room where they had the damaged painting set up for an artist to come in to try to restore. It had been rolled at a diagonal with a matte gray. The piano, which was done in gold leaf, and would have made a striking collegiate ensemble with the maroon, had the same gray color speckled all over it. It was worth getting mad over. Fred showed it all to me with a look that said, "What a shame," and he said it himself a time or two. Fred's wife, Stella, was out shopping; her favorite pastime, in his opinion, so I got no bead on her, but he said she had been especially nasty about it. I marked it down as a thing to remember, but it was tough to imagine a woman stabbing a man to death at his home. More likely a woman would have done that right then, while Scudder still held the gray covered paint roller in hand.

Ralph was having a nap in the car when I walked out, with his head propped on the door pillar, and his feet out the passenger window. I stood and looked enviously at him for a moment, before I pulled the back door open. He came to in no great hurry.

"Through already, John?" He started the motor. "Where to now?"

I looked in my notebook and read off the address to Dick Templeton's house.

The Templeton household, on the 3000 block of Union, in Bridgeport, was much less of a sprawl. It was just an apartment building. I left Ralph at the curb for another nap, and read over the names on the directory under a little awning. Templeton was listed on the second floor, so I went in and up. The whole place was brown with matching dirty carpet. I knocked on the door, and just answered, "Open up," through the door, to a woman's demand of, "Who is it?" from within.

She did open up, and didn't give me a shock, so much as something I didn't expect. A hundred dollars said the woman that cracked the door and peeked at me with her eye at the level of the chain was Dick Templeton's mother. He had been told to us as a guy hired just to carry paint, and unless he was a very unique specimen, I didn't expect him to have a wife with such pronounced crow's feet. I passed a card through the crack.

"John Trait. Private detective. Is Dick Templeton in?"

She held the card in the crack, as if she thought I didn't trust her with it, and looked it over. After a moment of study, she spoke.

"My son isn't in right now. He's at work."

I'll take my hundred in installments if necessary.

"You can keep that, Mrs. Templeton. I need to talk with him about his old boss, Roy Scudder. Where's Dick working now?"

Her mouth turned down.

"That's too bad about Roy. I hate that. He was so good to Dick. Taught him to drive. Dick's taken over the rest of the city jobs for Mr. Cline."

"Thank you, ma'am. The Park District, isn't it?"

"Yes, sir."

I thanked her again, and asked her to have him call me if I didn't see him first. She said she would, and I headed back down.

Ralph hadn't had time to count enough sheep, and had the motor running before I got to the door. I figured the parks building was on Dave's list, and so he might run into Templeton himself. I decided to save it for last. With him being the one that found the body, he had also won himself the most attention from the police, as they like to work from the point of closest proximity, and they had let him go back to work. Even still, a part of the puzzle was missing from my mind, and that was the crime scene itself. Where had Scudder fallen, how big was the knife, had there been any signs of a struggle, all that.

"Where to now?" Ralph asked, pulling the car from the curb. I had two first names on my notepad, and I switched from one to the other. Needing to give an order, I decided to work them out in the same order Roy Scudder had.

"Take me back north, Ralph." I gave him Sara Scudder's address. Roy's first wife.

CHAPTER FIVE

Never have I visited a more contrasting couple of leads. In my notes they looked the same. They received rings from the same man, bothered to stick around long enough to say they'd hang around a while, both decided that was a bad idea and went off looking elsewhere. Everyone has a type too, so you'd expect Roy Scudder to have picked from nearly the same rack, but if there had ever been parity between these two women, I couldn't see it.

Ralph pulled us up to a quaint little sided house that backed up to the west side of the Rosehill Cemetery. The huge green expanse, with its many paths, must have made for a pretty view from the back windows. Ralph nosed us into the drive and shut the motor off for another little wait. Sara Scudder's place had a small porch with a swing on the front. I climbed the steps and rang the bell. No interrogation from inside this time. The door just swung open.

"Hello there," she said, in a friendly voice. This was

our client's mother, and the resemblance was unmistak-
able. The look ahead did bode well for the daughter,
despite the narrow top half of the face that seemed heredi-
tary. She smiled at me. So, after introducing myself and
presenting my card, I chanced it to ask if I could come in.
She stood aside and let me do so.

It was a good looking little house, without too much
clutter, and reminded me of my folk's home. Conservative.
She set us up in the main sitting room, and turned down a
radio that she'd been listening to.

"You can just set that on the table, Mr. Trait."

I gathered up some crocheting that was under
construction, and placed it gently on a side table to free up
an end of the couch. I looked around for some small talk as
I took my seat and readied my notes.

"You must be very proud of your college girl, Mrs.
Scudder," I offered, observing a wall of pictures of my
client in various celebrations and activities on the Loyola
campus.

"Oh, yes, Mr. Trait. Sally is the first woman in my
family to go."

She was beaming at me, and that was a good sign. I
moved gently to business, though I didn't think she would
have hurt a fly.

"I'm here, at your daughter's hiring, to ask you some
questions concerning your ex husband."

I could have just saved my gentleness, because her
mood surely could not have regressed any more than it did.
Her mouth turned down, and her tone sharpened.

"What do you want to know?"

"Did he have any enemies?"

"Well, he had me." She just let it hang like that. We sat blinking at each other while I rearranged my thoughts. I hadn't expected that. At risk of getting ran out, and hoping she had deadpanned, I asked, "Well, did you kill him?"

Completely unmoved, she looked me dead in the face for a moment. A few blinks later, she spoke.

"Do you smoke, Mr. Trait?"

I said I did, and got out my pack. We each took one, and she sat a glass on the table for an ashtray. Now, with a somewhat different image, she talked between drags.

"I wouldn't have waited all these years to kill Roy Scudder. I had plenty of time, and opportunity, to do it while we lived in that ratty house. Listen, Mr. Trait. It's no surprise that our girl goes to that catholic university. We raised her- I raised her, to be a good Christian girl. That's how I was brought up, and Roy too." She flicked into the glass, inhaled again, and continued.

"You know, one night, God, fifteen years ago, maybe. Roy had come home drunk. He was supposed to have been at work, but had stopped at a liquor store so he wouldn't have to when he got off." She tilted her head toward me for an aside.

"That was always his play when he planned on missing work, you see. Anyway, he comes in with a bottle of cheap burgundy, and wants to tell me all about it. He said that he'd had one in the truck, and had brought the second for me. Said it tasted just like Communion when he was a boy. He said that was his first drink. He said, from that day, that he liked the drink so much he'd have to have another."

"So he was drinking when you met him?" I put in.

"He was as wet as a fish. He was fun though, and he always had a little money. We married young, and I figured he'd straighten out after a while. I was wrong."

I chuckled a bit. That last part came out to the beat of 'Que sera sera'.

"So, what about when Sally came along? No straighter?" I asked.

"Not a bit. The thing was that Roy was a friendly drunk. He was never the type to get down or mean. Even if he was just sitting in the shop by himself, he was happy. He was good with Sally and supported her completely. She was very fond of him. It's a shame what happened, but I can't say I'm surprised."

This was shaping up to be a strange interview. I admit I needed some hand holding, so I asked for it.

"I don't get it, Miss Scudder, if he was a nice guy, fun, all that, then why no surprise? Where did these enemies come from, and for that matter, what became your problem with him?"

She leaned back a bit with her cigarette and eyed me for a moment. She explained.

"It was the business where he made all the enemies. He was impulsive, as you might imagine, so he'd work for peanuts, because it'd put a bit of cash in his hand. That made the other painters upset, because he'd also go on stints where he'd work a lot. They'd show up in the driveway shouting at him for undercutting them. Then there were the customers. He'd go in some days and paint the wrong room, or use the wrong color. One time, he'd gone to the store on the front end, and decided to show up to the job anyhow. He talked his helper into sitting with him on the owner's couch and getting lit. The owners came home from their jobs and Roy and his man had ate all their food, and set a dish rag on fire cooking. That made for a few rounds in the driveway, too."

I took it down in my book as: History of altercations. But with all of it being so long ago, didn't bother to get names or addresses. The paint would have long since dried on those disputes, you might say.

"And what about you, Miss Scudder?"

"I couldn't take the inconsistency, Mr. Trait. You don't know what it's like to have someone around that can be so unpredictable, and sometimes, so careless."

Little did Sara Scudder know, I did in fact have a Roy Scudder in my life. Luckily for me, if I take a step away from the car annoyance, Dave's unpredictability usually panned out as a strength for our little agency, but I understood the sentiment. I wrapped up and got out of there. It was clear she didn't do it, didn't care enough to hire someone to do it, and didn't keep enough contact to know who might have done it. I had found out a good deal more about our victim, and felt more confident that checking the jobs in the black book was the best course of action.

Jumping to the next branch of the Scudder family tree, Ralph pulled us into a drive in West Roger's Park, just a

41

stone's throw away from our client's University. This one was a red brick house in a good neighborhood. I knocked on the door and got nothing. I knocked again, a little harder, and a man's voice called that he was on the way. The door opened to the limit of the chain, and a shirtless man appeared.

"We don't want any." He was snappy, but cordial. He laughed about it.

"I'm not selling any. You must be Wally."

He shut the door, removed the chain, and opened up. I was relieved to see his lower half covered.

"How'd you know?"

"Sally Scudder told me. Is Ellen home?"

Ed Wallace, Wally, for short, guffawed at the news, put his hand on his head, and said, "She's Ellen's daughter-in-law, or I guess she was. That's crazy."

I know my face must have shown my perturbation, but Wally wasn't the type to pick up on those kinds of things. He was more cut out for literally picking up things. To say he was strapping would have been an understatement. His clear deficiencies upstairs were made up for with a bruiser's frame. I only came up to his nose, and he wasn't wearing any shoes.

"Who is it, Wally?" came a voice from inside.

"I don't know yet, babe," he called back over his shoulder. He came back to me. "What do you want?"

I handed out another card and explained.

"My name is John Trait, with the David and Trait Detective Agency. Sally Scudder has hired my partner and

I to look into the death of her father, Roy. I understand you and he had contact?"

He'd been doing his best impression of a man that can read on my card, but at mention of Scudder, flicked it with two fingers out the door and over my left shoulder. I pretended not to care, and asked, "Do you mind if I come in and ask you all some questions?" I smiled, but was prepared to move, should he try to send my nose off in the same direction as the card.

He turned back over the shoulder again, and relayed, "He wants to talk some more about the fight, babe."

"What?" she shouted.

He repeated it.

She didn't hear it, again.

The whole thing, one more time.

"Can I just come in?" I nearly pleaded. He stood aside. "Thank you."

Wally, the guard dog, must not have had much hosting experience, and made me guess as to where the meeting would take place. It wasn't a huge house, and most of the lights were off, besides the room they were occupying. I found Ellen Scudder laid out on a chaise lounge, picking at a bowl of fruit, wearing a maroon silk robe, and generally trying to do her best Cleopatra. Wally was providing the scenery, and maybe had a palm fan tucked away somewhere. He took up a position behind her and stood. I pulled a chair around and got my notes out.

Ellen Scudder didn't make any sense to me. I mean, in context. She was simple enough to read as a singularity. The first wife, who I'd just been to, was probably forty-five;

fifty at the most, and was sliding on naturally toward eventual grandmahood. Here, keeping with the age old tradition, Roy Scudder had gone for a newer model on the second go. Ellen was forty at a push, had a frankly astonishing figure, and worked it for all it had.

She turned halfway, and let her hand rest near her hip, to see if she could move my eyes. I dodged the trap that Wally's eyes had set for me.

"Are you with the police?" she asked.

"No, ma'am. Private dick. John Trait. Sally Scudder hired me to look into the murder of your ex husband."

"I go to school with her, babe." Wally added that like it was helpful. He was roundly ignored.

"What do you want to know? Wally didn't kill him. He was fine when he left." She raised the hand up and touched Wally's face. She added, "My poor Wally got the worst of it."

"I don't suppose you all remember where you were that night, do you?" I asked plainly.

"I was here," she said. "By myself. The police came and asked me all about it. They said it happened late at night. I told them I was asleep, because I was."

Wally volunteered as soon as my eyes went to him.

"I was in Cudahy, studying."

"In the middle of the night? Is that a dormitory?"

"No, it's the library."

"Can anybody vouch for that?"

He puffed up, proudly. "Sure. Plenty of people. I figure Sally was probably there too."

I was torn. On one hand, I wanted to dress him down

for that terrible lie, right there. On the other, I wasn't sure I could take him without shooting him. After seeing him in person, I was putting the lick Scudder had got in down as a lucky shot. Also, Ellen wasn't giving me anything, and something about her eyes, which were intense if you looked hard enough, gave me the idea that I didn't want her turned against me. I put down to test the alibi, and moved on to another question.

"Miss Scudder, do you know of anyone that might have had it out for Roy?"

She worked a grape off the vine and ate it while she thought.

"I don't really keep up with Roy anymore, Mr. Trait. He was fun for a while, but then I saw he was so boring. Sally was fun, though." She smiled wide. It was a sign, and she meant it as one. The smile said, "My mouth is open, but my lips are sealed. Let's not waste anymore time." It was the look you give the overzealous vacuum salesman when he insists on going through with the demonstration.

I shut my notebook and bid them farewell, letting myself out, because Wally made no move for anything. I had a look into the other rooms as I went. They were all decorated in deep colors and plush fabrics. Romance seemed the intent of the design.

As we pulled into what was now the five o'clock traffic, I had a couple of things I could try. I directed Ralph to find me a phone, so I could check if Templeton had called the office. Twenty minutes of gridlock later, the call was made, and the report from Sid was a goose egg. Since we were in the area, I thought I'd bust Wally's alibi real quick, so I told Ralph to drive me to the campus.

Loyola University sits right on the shore of Lake Michigan, and the campus consists of just a few big red brick buildings. The most striking being the Madonna Della Strada chapel, with its bold stone front. It's not the jewel of the area, however. That honor would have to go to the Mundelein Tower that houses the women's school. At least that's my opinion. Ralph made sure to drive us up Sheridan, so he could see the two angels that flank the south entrance of the tower. They were worth the detour, as they stand reaching skyward, all the way to the third-story windows. With no sure idea where I would start, I told Ralph to let me out at the corner, by a building with, Cuneo Hall, on the front.

Five something on a Monday looked like a peak time for club activity, and the lawn and pathways that connected the buildings buzzed with activity. I stopped for a procession of runners as I made my way for the main building, and caught a few lines of Shakespeare being read in parts by a group of youths on the grass. The dress code, if there was one, had one clear item on it, and that was everything was maroon and gold; the Rambler's colors. I had expected some school spirit, but it was a sight none the less. Further on I saw something I hadn't expected. David DeGrabber, sticking out in his usual dark blue jacket, standing in the grass, looking intently on an artist who had gathered quite a crowd as he painted a large work.

CHAPTER SIX

D ave does this weird thing- Ah, who am I kidding? Dave's weird, and sometimes, if he knows you, he doesn't think it necessary to make any acknowledgement when you come into the room, or in this case, walk up beside him. We stood, silently, and watched the guy paint. It was a show, at every level, and the artist was determined to be the center of it. He had on a maroon kind of tunic and a gold belt, like an Indian might wear. He wore his hair far too long, so he painted with his right and habitually brushed it back with his left. It was dark black. He was working a pretty big brush on a canvas, that I estimated at seven feet by four feet, with slashing strokes. Right now he was detailing a figure, maybe an angel or goddess, on a field of stars, in deep red. To make drama, I guess, he seethed or shouted with every few strokes, as if he were having trouble with the thing. He was doing a lot of moving and shouting, for not a lot of picture, I thought. The whole thing was too dark for my taste, and I couldn't see anybody wanting something like that around.

"Elsa," the painter called, without looking from his work. "Prepare me a celestial gold, with a gash of red."

A girl who did not look like she fit in as a student, but must have been, sprung to action. She had the tunic look going on too.

"Yes, Bartholomew," she cried, as if she'd disappointed him by not foreseeing his demand. I had to look at the ground for a second, it was all so cheesy. He told her to hurry, as though he needed her to ready another pint of blood for surgery. She took a couple tubes of color from a big satchel on the ground and emptied them onto a board. She mixed those around frantically, and held the red over her head with both hands, and squeezed a gob down on top of the, "celestial gold". He turned to her to accept the offering, and she presented it as such, with bowed head and everything. He looked at the board, took it in his left like a drinks tray, sampled the mixture with his finger- in his mouth, I couldn't believe it either- and then, now just finger painting, wiped an arc of gold with red in it around the figure, like a halo or aura. Bartholomew stood back from his creation, somehow decided it was perfect, turned to the group of onlookers, and shouted as he raised his hands aloft in victory. People clapped. I just shook my head.

Dave had not been unmoved either. He was applauding, though refrained from any whooping. It was a good time to get back to work.

"I guess I just like my art to look like something," I stated.

"It is like a magician's act, John," Dave offered, following me toward the central building.

"I didn't see any cards or rabbits."

I held the door to the Jesuit Residence building, and went in after Dave.

The campus interiors weren't nearly as crowded as outside, and we found a corridor of offices on the first floor in no time. I knocked on one that said, Administrations, on it, and poked my head in.

"How may I help you?" said a fat man behind a little desk. He was in conference with a professor. I could tell by the smug pretentiousness that came out of him. It's not that all professors are that way, maybe not even half, but it's never hard to find one in a group.

I walked in quick and stuck my hand out, so they wouldn't have time to tell me to wait outside.

"John Trait. Detective. This is my partner, David DeGrabber. One of your students hired us to look into something, and we need to check on an alibi. You've got a good idea what all goes on around here, don't you?"

"I should hope so. Have a seat, Mr. Trait. Professor Etchwilde, and I, were just finishing up."

"Oh, may I ask, professor of what?" That was Dave. Something was up. I'm sure, to them, he sounded polite and engaged, and he did, but for Dave, he might as well have been giddy. Etchwilde The Pretentious gave his entire resume.

"I am Loyola's director of the fine arts. Masters from

Cambridge with a primary focus in oils." He sat with one leg over the other, and looked up at the ceiling and blinked fast as he spoke.

"Ah. We have just come in from witnessing a spectacle by one of your pupils," Dave said.

Etchwilde scoffed. Twice. He looked around the top of the walls for something, and then let us in on it.

"Bart Henry is no pupil of mine. Abusing canvases, and caking paint into his brushes. He's an animal. That vaudeville, he calls art, is of a different world than myself, or my craft."

I'd taken a fair feeling leather chair, and as tired as I was getting, made no effort to hide what a bunch of belly-aching it all was to me. I wasted no grace returning the discussion to where we needed it.

"Well, one of the students here told me he'd been in the library in the early morning hours of a Saturday night, a month ago. Does that sound likely to you?"

Clandon, as it said on a plaque on his desk, scoffed just one time.

"That's as good an excuse as any. Have you been hired to chase after some student's romantic partner? They're not supposed to have them, but we can't stop them."

"No, I imagine they're hard enough to teach painting to. So you don't think the library angle is very likely?"

"No, Mr. Trait. I wish it were. For this entire last semester the campus has been a ghost town on the weekend evenings, because of certain get-togethers that have been taking place somewhere off campus."

I pulled out my pad and pencil.

"Where exactly are these get-togethers?"

He looked down at his desktop and laid both palms on it. "We don't know, Mr. Trait. We would like to, however, hiring detectives would be a decision for the dean, or maybe a committee. By then, I expect word will have gotten to us."

"I can give it to you on the house, if you'll point me in a direction to look."

He raised the palms to heaven. "All I can think, is it must be within walking distance, because far fewer students drive than seem to disappear on the weekends."

Dave had one and asked it. He'd put his cheer away and was himself again.

"Mr. Clandon, you hired a painter to do a job, here on the campus, through the Park District last week, yes?"

Clandon turned his eyes over to Dave, and seemed to wonder why the segue.

"I did. The work was done today, in fact."

"May we see the site, Mr. Clandon?"

"I guess so." Clandon got to his feet, revealing that he was only five two. He took a little case from under his desk, tucked it under his arm, and said, "I'm done for the day, anyway. We can talk some more tomorrow, if you need to, Eric." The professor nodded like it was a bow and left us. Clandon turned off some lights and moved a few things around before he locked the door.

"Follow me," he announced.

The campus was a little quieter now, with the sun beginning to set. Clandon led us down a northbound path, past the library, and around back of it. We didn't use the path that ran around the northern perimeter of the building, and instead took to the grass and down a little decline. A little ways away from the lake, we came to a depression where the foundation of the library stood as a block wall.

"Here it is. It was only some vandalism. I'm going to head home. I'll be back in my office tomorrow, if you have any more questions. Good luck."

Dave stopped him with a quick one.

"Do you know who painted over the thing, Mr. Clandon?"

He stopped and thought hard for a second, placing a knuckle to his head.

"Templeton, I think it was. He came and told me it was finished."

Dave thanked him, and we bade him farewell. He waddled off across the grass, and up a little knoll.

"Not much to see," I observed. It was just a gray wall, with a fresher gray place in the middle, about four feet in diameter.

Dave had his arms crossed. He stared at it broodingly and said nothing. I looked at him, since I'd seen the wall, and tried to decide if he had taken a nap while I'd been riding around with Ralph. It was a tough call.

"I've not been able to see one of these yet today," he finally said, turning to go. I followed.

"Able to see one of what?" I asked.

He fluttered a hand with his answer. No nap.

"The graffiti. I went to four of them, and they had all been well covered. I haven't been able to make them out."

"Gosh, Dave, there's probably all kinds of people

painting crap on walls. You don't think that has anything to do with our dead painter, do you?"

"They're all a similar size," he offered.

It wasn't nothing, but darned close. I yawned.

"I think we need to try again tomorrow."

"Let's check one more."

He stopped and pulled out the black notebook. I looked over his shoulder at the addresses.

"Let's take this one," I suggested, pointing to an entry. "It's close to Carl's shop. I told him to expect me tonight. We can get our suitcases."

Dave liked that idea, and asked if I still had a cab. I told him Ralph was still billing the client, so we hoofed it back off campus. Ralph gave Dave the cold shoulder, on my behalf, as we motored south down Lakeshore, using up the last of the daylight. Carl's shop was near the bottom edge of the loop, so I let Ralph go once he dropped us off.

"About time you made it," came a gruff voice from under a black pickup hood. I can't understand how Carl's voice ever got so much gravel in it, as he was only a year or so older than myself, and kept no damaging habits.

"We've been working to pay for the bill you're gonna make for us," I said.

He sat a wrench down and held out a greasy hand. I went ahead and shook it. Carl is a big man, both in height and width, with heavy hands; good for turning bolts, bad for handling the small nuts. I only bring him in on matters I deem beyond my knowhow, or that I don't have the tools for. I had met him in Europe, where he wrenched on tanks, trucks, and artillery, for a few seasons, and we became friends as men willing to tackle any job. He was like Dave and I, in a way. He could have gone to a factory, or worked for the city waiting on someone to retire to take their seat, but instead he came back from helping stop the blitz, and opened his own humble shop. Business was up and down, like it was for us, and though he complained about it either way, you could tell he was glad no one told him what to do.

"What's the diagnosis on the Dave-mobile?" I inquired.

He answered matter-of-factly. "Haven't touched it yet. Got three in front of it."

I knew better than to ask. It's a mechanic's universal policy to take in all the cars they can get, and work on as many as they can, before people start taking them somewhere else off the far end of the line. A lot of time they won't, as that would require another tow fee, and the next shop probably has just as long a line.

"Just let us know as soon as you know something." I added a grin to remind him we were friends.

Our chat was going on through the open bay door, of which Carl had two. Dave hadn't moved from the spot on the curb that the cab had dropped us on. He thumbed through the painter's notebook, studying intently.

"How far is the next stop?" I asked him.

"Two blocks east," he said, pointing down the street.

I turned back to Carl. "Are you gonna be around for a little while longer?"

"Nope. Wife's got dinner waiting."

I shrugged. We all tend to have a master, despite our efforts.

"All right, let me get into the car real quick."

Carl went for the key, and I got the two suitcases from the trunk. They weren't large, but Dave's was heavier than I wanted to carry. I brought it to the curb and sat it under where his hand would go. He took it up, and started down the darkened sidewalk. I told Carl I'd talk to him soon. He was already turning lights out and waved.

Dave led the way, with the notebook in his off-hand. It was a wonder he didn't walk into a pole, with the way he continued to stare at it as we went. He held up a little at an alleyway, and then started off again. I happened to look down the passage.

"Dave, look there." I tried to be quiet, but urgent. He stopped and looked. There was a man, probably sixty yards into the alley. The hiss of a spray can could just be heard, and the arm held out, though obstructed by poles, garbage receptacles, signs, and things, gave it away that this was one of the city's outlaw artists at work.

Before we had time to confer about it, the vandal spotted us and ran. Dave gave no word, only dropped his suitcase where he stood, and bolted down the alley after him.

"Nuts," I exclaimed, mostly to myself. I switched hands with my case, gathered Dave's, and took off in pursuit. Dave was moving well, and it was all I could do to stay within a helpful distance. The vandal had turned left at the other end, and was out of my sight when I made the corner. Dave still had a bead on him and didn't hold up. He dashed down a path between a building and a railway fence, for maybe ten strides, and hung another left. I held the cases high by my shoulders to give my legs more room to work. I heard Dave shout at our quarry, and then to me, as I started to turn in on the second left.

"Keep straight, John!" he boomed.

I aborted the turn in, disturbing my cargo's inertia, and kicked hard in the way I'd been going. Dave had made a right, and I could see him intermittently now. I became aware that I was passing garages, behind apartment houses, and Dave and our subject were jumping fences at intervals as they dashed through the yards.

The houses ran out before I had run completely out of breath, and our man turned back my way. He dashed by me, and I might have tackled him, had I not had my hands full. By the look I got, he was wearing all black, buttoned up high, with a hat pulled as low as it would go. He had on a small backpack that matched the rest of the ensemble. I had to turn a stride into a leap to miss Dave as he blew by in pursuit.

"Send him back this way!" I shouted.

The lead he had on me allowed for some strategy. Before me, illuminated by a single back alley street light, was a clear smooth runway, and our man had gone over the single train track, and was going between more garages and houses. Dave shouted to the affirmative, and ran out to the front of the buildings, so he'd have a clear run to get ahead. I put my head down, pulled the suitcases up as high as I could, and got the wind whistling by my ears.

The next crossing came, and I looked for Dave, or our mark. Nothing. I dug deep for another push, and stomped to a stop on the other side of the next crossing. It was another alley. I looked back the way I came, and each way of the crossing, but couldn't see anybody, then heard footsteps behind me. I wheeled around, ready to jettison the cases, but it was only Dave, trotting into the alley from the other side.

I gulped some air, and said, "Did we lose him?"

Now I was convinced Dave had taken a nap, because he answered with no great difficulty.

"It seems so. Dammit!" He stomped his foot and turned around.

I shushed him, and sat the suitcases down carefully.

"You hear that?" I whispered. "In the dumpster."

It was halfway down the alley, with the lids closed. We stalked up to it, and knowing it may just be a cat, or a rat, I spared no caution and readied fists. Dave flipped the lid.

"You'll never take me!" came a shout from within.

I did take him, though. I aimed a right hand at where the sound had come from, found a shirt collar, and yanked him from the hiding place. He pawed at my arms as I ushered him toward the light back at the end of the alleyway.

"Not him," I complained, releasing the man. In the light it was clear he was just a dirty bum. I started to ask why he had hid, but he scampered off as soon as I let go. I groaned, looking at my jacket cuffs, at the God knows what he had slathered on them in his struggles.

"Can we go home now?" I pleaded.

Dave didn't answer. He had moved to the mouth of the alley, and was scanning back and forth. After a moment he started walking, so I gathered the cases again, and followed.

"Here. Do I look like a bellhop?" I shoved his bag into his hand, and transferred mine to my strong hand, which didn't help much, because my arms were jelly after the run.

"We're here," Dave stated. We had only walked a half block, and turned back toward the tracks. They went over a drain of some kind, and so had a good-sized concrete block supporting wall on either side of a pipe.

"They're here too," I observed. The Chicago Police had lights, cars, men, and equipment, around the scene. A section of wall was missing, and blocks were being arranged into piles, and flash photography was being taken. Dave pulled the notebook out again and tried to get some light on it, I presume to check if it was, in fact, the spot.

We made our way toward the fray, and in the direction of a face we knew.

"The train station is further down. You two going on a trip?" It was Detective Ben Scott, with Chicago Homicide.

CHAPTER SEVEN

Between the sleep in the car, waking up at dawn, a day of traveling to and fro to suspects, and the chase through the alleyways, I was beat and nearly spilled it to Scott, right then and there, why it was we had walked up on his crime scene. I caught it, however, and found myself back in the office the next day, after a decent night's sleep and a morning shave and shower. Dave had done likewise. We each sat at our desks.

Another call was put in to Mrs. Templeton, but the painter's helper, now just the new painter, had left for work bright and early. His mother said she would let him know to contact us, but I started to feel strung along in that she acted on the phone like she'd never heard of me, or any member of my profession, for that matter.

Dave was working through the morning Tribune, and addressed me from the other side of it.

"Another girl has gone missing," he mumbled.

"Sally Scudder mentioned that, didn't she?"

He folded the sheets over twice and lobbed them to me. It held together well enough and I corralled it. The story wasn't enough to be worth repeating here. Just a call, from a Mr. and Mrs. Archie Carnes, for information concerning the whereabouts of their daughter, Amanda, age 20. They'd even spent the extra on a picture, and she pleased the eye from what could be seen in black and white.

I was looking the headshot over, trying out different colored shirt collars and hair in my mind, when a knock at the door brought my eyes up. It was clear through the frosted window who our visitor was, and no surprise that Sid hadn't forewarned us. Detective Scott likes to threaten Sid with obstruction, which was just bloviating, of course, but Sid won't risk it.

"Come in," Dave beckoned from his chair.

I started to get up, but Scott handled the door, and skipped the coat rack, like always. He took a chair from the wall, sat it near us at the end of the desks, and sank into it. He was in the same heavy brown overcoat as he had on the night before, and all the times I'd seen him before that. It made him look both wider and shorter than he actually was, though I think he would be better served in something slimming. He didn't say anything at first, and just looked from me and then to Dave, spending more time on Dave, with his big bright red mustache shifting from side to side as he considered where to start.

"All right, DeGrabber," he began slowly. "What are you two working on?"

Dave was sat low in his chair with his legs stretched

out beyond the underside of his desk. He started contentiously enough, though he spoke with the bored tone he often used.

"Detective Scott, wouldn't you think it improper if John and I approached you about your affairs, with no provocation?"

Scott was patient. He considered another moment and went at it again.

"I do not buy that you and John were just walking around with your suitcases, and happened to come across that out of the way piece of train track. I tell you, what we found there, last night, has me in the mood to bargain a little. What'll it take to get the dope?"

Dave crossed his arms and slid up in his chair. For the first time so far he cut his eyes over to Scott.

"I offer a trade. An outline of our current case in exchange for the details, as you and your men have gathered them, on the stabbing death of Roy Scudder."

Scott's head jerked back in surprise at the request.

"That's all?" Dave nodded slightly. Scott raised his shoulders and let them back down. He sounded relieved and gave it up.

"Well, that one's still open, but there's not much to it. I think I remember it pretty well from the report. I didn't see to it personally."

"Why was that?" Dave interjected.

Scott turned his hands up.

"I'm busy, all right? Anyhow, Scudder was found dead in his garage, stabbed, like you said, on Sunday morning, by a helper. They were supposed to finish up a job for the Park District. The Medical Examiner put the time of death around midnight or one. No sign of struggle really, even though he was stabbed high in the belly. It's tough to say if he didn't fight back because he knew the guy, or if he was too lit to. He'd been drinking late that night, as he did most nights. That's pretty much the bag."

"Where in the garage was he killed?" Dave followed up.

"Right by the door. We think, somebody knocks, Scudder answers it, and gets it right there. He falls back into the pathway, by the drop cloths, and expires from blood loss."

"I'm surprised it didn't get on the drop cloths," I commented.

"Well, I guess I don't have to ask what you're working on, or for who. That daughter of his has called my office at least a dozen times in the last month, but I just don't have anything to tell her. No fingerprints, and the ex wives, and their boyfriends, are all clean."

I made a smirk of disbelief. "You're calling Ed Wallace clean?"

"That's what it says in my report."

I stayed incredulous. "Ben, who do you have working this case, anyway? I talked to Ed Wallace yesterday, and checked his alibi. It's as flimsy as those drop cloths. Also, the first wife doesn't look like she's got a man, unless you do know something we don't."

The ends of Scott's mustache turned toward the floor, and his jaw set.

"I've had Jefferson on it. You say that alibi isn't any good?" he muttered.

"You'd never let it pass, Ben," I empathized.

He exhaled deeply.

"What of the murder weapon? Do you have it?" Dave wondered.

"I don't know for sure. I'll find out more about it when I get back to the station. We have a trade to finish, though. What part of this Scudder thing brought you and Trait to that horror show behind that wall last night?"

Dave answered plainly.

"We were checking a work history of Roy Scudder."

"He'd been there? When?" Scott asked.

"Unclear. The book we have has no dates. Roy Scudder, and his helper, had many job locations listed for the Park District. We believe those on plain walls were to cover up graffiti. Was there such a work on that wall last night?"

Scott looked down and shook his head. He wasn't himself. Scott's never exuberant, but hardly ever downtrodden, so I ventured an inquiry.

"What was behind that wall, Ben?"

He brought his eyes up to mine, and I could see some red in them. He looked tired.

"It was bad, John. No artwork. We think we have the body of a young female. Someone had taken out a couple of the concrete blocks, cleared some space behind them, stuffed her in it, and put the blocks back in. Well, just the fronts of the blocks. I guess he needed the room or something. The lab guys are sorting all that out now."

SHANE CHASTAIN

"My God," I exclaimed.

"Alive?" Dave asked plainly.

Scott shook his head some more.

"Oh, no. Certainly not. She had been," Scott paused to consider. He grimaced as he finished the thought. "altered to fit."

"Any idea who she was?" I asked.

Another shake of the head.

"It looks like she'd been there a while. They're working on the I.D. downtown." Scott had a faraway look in his eyes, and now rattled his head around and came back to us. "Well, your painter and my girl may just be a coincidence, but I'll find out more about both when I talk to Jefferson. I probably said too much about this girl. Keep it under your hat, all right?"

The phone rang. Scott slapped his hands on his knees and hoisted himself up. Dave picked up the call, and I got up to get the door. At the door I asked Ben, "Are you all right, buddy?"

He shrugged.

"I'll be fine tomorrow. After digging her out so late, I made the wife sit up with me and play some cards. Try to keep DeGrabber's nose out of anything messy, will ya?"

I told him I would do my best, and held the door. Dave was finishing the call, an appointment booking by the sound of it, as I returned to my chair, stowing the extra one Scott had used on the way, to keep things tidy.

"Templeton or Scudder?" I guessed.

"Archie Carnes."

I whistled low.

"They'll be here in an hour," Dave added.

The hour was spent with the radio on, and my trying to tease yesterday's movements out of Dave. The case of whether or not Dave had taken a nap was still unclear, and seemed as though it would remain as such indefinitely. He had not, in fact, gone to the Park District building, so I made a note to myself to check on it the next time I made my way downtown. I also gave him all I could on my findings, before the intercom sounded.

"I'm bringing a couple up." It was Sid's voice, crackling through the speaker from his desk downstairs. I hopped up and sat two of the best looking client's chairs up on the rug, one at the end of each of our desks. Dave rummaged around in a drawer, and produced a fresh notepad that he probably wouldn't use. I strolled to the door to greet our guests, and opened up as I heard the elevator doors shut and Sid start back down. The Carnes came down the hallway with a look of stiffly disguised uncertainty, common among the well-to-do's that visit our humble office. I greeted them with a smile and ushered them through the door. Though it wasn't the time of year for overcoats, I took one from the man, and a fur thing from the lady, and hung them carefully from our rack. I can only assume they had dressed for any circumstance that might befall them on their safari into the commonwealth.

Archie and Rebecca Carnes were steeped in wealth and stodginess. They were familiar to me, in reputation, from social pages, as well as billboards around the city that advertised Carnes Manufacturing, of which this Mr. Carnes had inherited from the last heir. Their address had been printed in the paper, in the story about their daughter, and it was not in an area I had much opportunity to frequent. Mr. Carnes was midway through his sixties, and had come with a wife that could have been sold to me as twenty years his junior, but was really no more than ten years younger. He had on an expensive suit with stripes that went forever, with him being so tall. The lady was well covered in a royal blue dress, that though clearly expensive, was conservative and understated.

"If you two will have a seat, I'm John Trait, and this is David DeGrabber." They looked down their noses at the chairs, but sat anyway. I settled in myself and continued. "How may we help you today?"

Mr. Carnes, all lanky six foot six of him, sat bolt upright, and spoke as though he was trying not to move his lips.

"We would like to hire you to find our daughter, Amanda."

The lady reached over and clung to his upper arm, as though he had done a great thing. Dave and I sat for a beat, thinking he might say anything more, but he seemed to have laid it out fully, in his mind.

"Well, Mr. Carnes, that's a succinct way to put it," I admitted. "We'll need some more information though. When did your daughter go missing? Where from? Things like that."

He took a sharp breath and let it back out.

"Amanda left ten days ago, the Saturday before last. She was supposed to have joined us at our lake house for the weekend, but phoned Friday evening that she had studies to attend to and would not be able to make it. At the time it was no great disappointment, as her studies are important, but then when we returned home, Sunday evening, a letter had come for us, from Amanda, saying that she would not be returning home, or to campus. We've not heard from her since."

"Do you have this letter?" Dave asked.

Carnes' head pivoted to his wife and tilted down a degree. She hurried into a bag in her lap and produced an envelope. She passed it to Dave.

"Where was Miss Carnes enrolled?" I asked.

"Mundelein College, sir," he answered.

The coincidences were beginning to pile up a little too quickly. I hadn't been near Loyola University at all before yesterday, or the Mundelein Women's college, with its guardian angels, and now it looked like two cases in as many days would take me to the area. Dave had finished reading and passed me the letter and envelope. I asked another question before I started on it.

"Why do you think she went missing on Saturday, if you received word from her on Sunday?"

I saw why as he answered.

"The postmark on the letter. It is stamped Saturday evening, and arrived in the Sunday morning post."

"From the college mail room," I observed.

"Yes, sir. A man at one of the other agencies made the point to us," he added.

My eyes had began to scan the letter, but I stopped for a moment. "You've talked with other detective agencies?"

Archie Carnes gave one big nod, and said, "Yes, sir. We have hired all the agencies in the city."

I let my hands, and the letter, drop to my knees.

"Today?"

Another single nod. "Yes, sir. We shall spare no expense."

Their money, I thought. I pulled the letter back up and gave it a read. It was a short one. Here's what it said, in type.

Dear, Mother and Father

I am leaving and do not expect to return home or to the college. I have been called to greater things and wish you well.

Amanda

Even the signature was typed. At my looking up and being up to speed, Dave took off around the next turn.

"Did you and your daughter have any difficulty in your home life?"

"Oh, my," squeaked Mrs. Carnes.

Dave rolled his eyes and turned himself a little more to face the couple.

"It is a valid question, Mrs. Carnes. Surely it has been indicated to you, by one of the many agencies you've engaged this morning, that these two typed lines may not be the words of your daughter. We know it not a complete hoax only by the fact that she has been absent, as indicated. We must still, however, endeavor to prove that it is a valid statement, made by her. I ask again, did your daughter have any great impetus to leave?"

Archie Carnes wasn't the, 'Oh, my-ing', type, but might as well have been. He was playing some sort of stiff upper lip act that would have fit right in beside Chamberlin. We weren't in England though, and the war was over. Dave didn't have any patience for the answer he got.

"I don't believe so, Mr. DeGrabber," was all Carnes said.

Dave had held his notepad this whole time, though I don't think he'd marked a page. He held it over his desk and let it drop with a thud. He looked straight at Archie's eyes, trying to convey his annoyance by expression, or telepathy. Maybe Carnes had never seen anybody act that way to him before, I don't know, but he certainly didn't seem to know what to do with it. They stared at one another for an uncomfortable twenty seconds. I decided that was a good enough stand off, and tried to move things along.

"Mr. Carnes, do you have the names of any of your daughter's friends, professors even, somebody we could talk to that she might have told something to?"

The staring contest, that Carnes didn't seem to know he was in, was broken, and he turned to me and thought a moment. Something came together, and he swung casually to the wife, and asked, "Rebecca, who was that young lady

Amanda spoke of last summer? The one that came to dinner."

The wife had the answer right away, and I thought maybe we'd have been better off with her, on her own, but she spoke so quietly, and not at all to us, that I decided Dave would run her off, so passed on it.

"That was Julia Stile," she nearly whispered.

I took it down, and asked her to spell it, but she couldn't and whispered something about how the Stile's aren't a well known family. I managed to get that Julia had dark hair, and was one of her daughter's classmates at Mundelein.

"The two of you were together for the entire weekend?" Dave asked blankly.

The couple looked at one another, and then back to Dave as though he'd lobbed a pie into their laps. They answered in unison.

"Yes."

When the Carnes left, after another fifteen minutes of administrative questions by me, they had officially hired, and retained, every detective agency in the city. I can't say they left feeling terribly confident, but then they hadn't walked in any better. Since we had been the last stop, it was a safe bet that none of the other dicks had worked any magic either. I went for $200 down, as we had done the day before, and got it. I might have left it till the very end though, because Mrs. Carnes' bag had a collection of checks already made out for $500, and they had to write a fresh one for our bargain pricing.

I let the aristocrats out, having buzzed down to Sid to

have the elevator elevated and waiting, got them re-coated, and bid them farewell. I had a stretch and a yawn while I read my watch.

"It's three now," I announced. "What do you say I head over and talk to the college friend, and see what we can drum up? The other agencies will probably wait till tomorrow, at least. You want to come along?"

Dave made me stand there for about thirty seconds. He just sat there motionless with his arms crossed, staring at the vacated client's chair in front of my desk, where the lady had been. Finally, he sat up, opened his desk drawer for a rifling, grabbed something, stood, and said,

"I'm going to keep checking Roy Scudder's job sites. I hope to run across his helper, Templeton, also."

With that, he hurried out the door. I checked my pockets for all necessary detective gear; pistol, paper, pencil, and money. It was all there, so I shut off the lights and locked up the office for the time being.

CHAPTER EIGHT

An idea came to me as I made my way down and out onto the sidewalk. I walked the mile and a half back to my apartment and climbed the four flights to my door. Inside my little apartment, which is just a main room and a bathroom, I dove into my closet. What I was searching for hadn't had much wear in some time, as v-necked sweaters have fallen out of my favor. It was there in the back, however, with no signs of insect predation. I shook it out a few times, discarded my tie for the evening, and pulled it on. The maroon sweater did look good in the mirror on the closet door. I patted my pockets and looked around for anything else that might help me, decided I had all I could get, and went back down to hail a cab to take me back up Lakeshore to the Loyola and Mundelein campuses.

Just so you know, the retrieval of the maroon sweater wasn't for anything so fanciful as impersonating a student. Though I wouldn't be quite a full decade removed from a college term, if I had taken one, those kids looked young.

The idea was, if I could blend in, just a little, then maybe I wouldn't get hampered or hassled by any of the staff, and might move more freely. Also, I thought the sympathetic color could have some subliminal effect on whoever I needed to question.

"Take it easy, will ya?" I complained in the cab.

I didn't like this cabbie anything like Ralph. The traffic was heavy, and he followed a little too close, and drove a bit too fast for my liking. It seemed he also had some kind of insurance that he was looking to make a claim on, if only he could find a pothole that would finish off the last of his cab's suspension. He only grunted in response to my commentary, and lined up another crater. Luckily, the angels of Mundelein were in sight, so I told him to pull over and let me out. He did, and I paid him, but held on to the tip.

I stopped in front of the doors to the tower, and admired the pair of statues as I considered where to start. There was no guarantee that Julia Stile was even in the tower, or on the grounds of either campus. I also had no description of Miss Stile, other than the Carnes' assertion that the name wouldn't mean much to anybody, and I didn't put much stock in their assessments of anything. Deciding that any place was as good as the next to start, I pulled the door and head in.

The Mundelein Tower is a striking thing from the outside, and no less so on the inside; laid out like a big bank lobby. A desk in the middle was unoccupied. My watch said 5:00, so I checked a building directory for a place to find some bodies. The second floor cafeteria stuck out, so I found an elevator and went up.

Girls were milling around, and sitting in groups talking. Other women were preparing the line for service. It was a near exclusively female crowd, and I didn't feel so much out of place, as I just knew a good few suspicious eyes were on me, some of which would be intent to make it tough sailing. Whether it be in an office, a nursery, or a school of any kind, a man can always run in to a large group of women. In my line of work it happens all the time. Similar to how the new lion has to approach and challenge the old, strong lion for entrance into the group, I picked out the loudest girl I could find.

The tables had fixed benches down both sides, picnic style, and she was sat with her green skirt on the top, and her feet on the bench, holding court over some eight or nine others that sat below her. She was pretty enough, with a round face and blonde hair that went down well beyond her shoulders. The mouth was her strongest feature, though. Not the shape of it, or anything like that, just that she used it. As I walked up she boomed about, "... What happened next..." I got her eye and waited for a breath. I piped up to match her volume.

"Hi, there. I'm trying to find Julia Stile."

Everybody laughed like it was the funniest joke they'd ever heard. After a moment the loud one said, "Well, I'm right here, silly." She held out a hand over the top of another girl for me to shake. It was awkward, but I couldn't afford to not make friends, so we shook over the top of a brunette who could have ran the whole tower, if she could just find some more amperage for her loud-speaker.

"What do you want to talk about? Mister?"

"John Trait. Private detective," I announced to ooo's and ahhh's. "I'm trying to track down Amanda Carnes. Have any of you seen her?"

A single line formed between Julia's eyebrows. She spoke.

"I haven't seen her since she started hanging around with that cult."

"It's not a cult, Jules," one of the girls stated.

"Is it not, Barb?" Julia said. "What else do you call it? Spending time out in the woods, and doing whatever those boys say. And how weird are they, anyway? It's a cult if ever I heard of one. I mean, they're leaving school for it!"

I got in fast.

"How many girls do you know that have been in this thing?"

She smirked. "It's hard to say. They go in and out. Barb went out with them a couple of times. Didn't you, Barb?" Barb nodded. She went on. "I don't know how many have left college over it. Amy was the only one I knew before Amanda."

I went ahead and got my notebook out, which had a marked effect on the air of the room.

"What's Amy's last name?"

She said it was Merkle, so Amy Merkle got added to my growing list of names with not much else.

"You said some men are in charge of this group. Do you know who they are?"

"I don't know if they're in charge of it, per se, but Bart Henry and Wally Wallace are the biggest recruiters I know."

Now I had some things to add to the names. I placed a couple gentle fingers on Barb's shoulder, and asked her, "Where do these get-togethers take place?"

She turned toward me with an embarrassed expression, and said, "They move around. I'm afraid I don't know. I just went the one time, you see. It was late, and I didn't really pay much attention. I'm not so good with directions, and that's even in the daytime."

I pulled the fingers off, and so stopped her potential filibuster. I told her it was ok. Back to Julia.

"You've not seen anything of Amanda, since when?"

"I talked to her the Friday before they say she left, in class."

"How did she seem?"

"Fine as ever."

"Did she send you a letter, or say anything to you about going for good?" I asked.

"No, sir. What's going on out there?"

Just like that, I lost the room. A girl at a south facing window had asked another to come look, and now I could scarcely get a view out of it myself, for the crowd that gathered around. Down below, pulled up to the curb on Sheridan Street, was a Chicago Police Car with three others just like it. It was unoccupied. The cafeteria doors swung open. I wheeled around to look. Ben Scott, with a half dozen city employees, stood in the threshold, surveying the scene.

Ben used the same strategy I had in determining who, out of the chattering masses that now stood behind me at the window, to try to get something useful out of. He pointed a stubby finger at the loud one, Julia, and motioned her to step forward. He addressed her loud enough that he might elicit a volunteer, if he were lucky.

"Do you know Amy Merkle?" he asked. Julia said she did, and Scott came right in with, "When was the last time you saw her?"

Julia looked back to me for something, but I didn't have it. "A couple months ago. Just before she left, I guess."

Scott asked for her name, got it, and gave some directions.

"We'll need you to come downtown for questioning, Miss Stile." He motioned with his head, and a uniformed officer approached to usher Julia out. Naturally, she protested.

"I don't have to go anywhere with you. What the hell is going on here?" she demanded.

The young cop tried to take her arm, and she pulled away and took a swat at him. He grabbed for her again, and she screamed, which put the rest of the gang into hysterics. I stepped to Ben to try to get a handle on the situation. We spoke under the cacophony.

"What's going on here, Ben?" I asked.

He checked both shoulders, leaned in for there to be no chance of anyone overhearing, and whispered, "That girl in the wall was Amy Merkle, a student here, and an open missing persons file."

I say there was no chance for eavesdropping, but

possibly the change in my expression spoke louder than the ruckus around us. Julia had her eyes on me, maybe hoping I'd jump in and pull her from the lawman. I looked over to her, and seeing on my face it wasn't good news, she relaxed, and allowed herself to be guided through the doors and down to a car.

"Does anybody else have knowledge of Amy Merkle?" Scott inquired. Nobody said a word, of course. I had an idea to try to stick with the action, and made my play on it as Scott turned and started for the next checkpoint.

"Ben. Let me ride with you to the station."

"Not a chance, Trait." He wasn't too nasty about it. I pressed into the elevator with him.

"I have some names I'll trade you. They're important, and they're right here. You could get them now, before word gets out and they fly."

The elevator doors opened, and he stamped out with me on his heels, then stopped. We were in the doorway of the tower, flanked by the stone angels. Scott looked over my head at one, and then behind him at the other, as if he had never noticed them before, sighed like he needed a night's sleep, and said, "Fine."

It would have been asking a lot for Ben to let me sit in on the interviews with Henry, Wallace, and Stile. Dave and I had finagled our way into the interview rooms at Michigan Avenue before, but that was on a stretch of attorney client privilege; Ben doesn't like lawyers. He might also have just gotten up on a different side of the bed that day. This particular evening he put me on ice straight away.

"Have a seat," he said as we entered the second floor closet that the chief made Ben call an office. I moved one of the many stacks of files that littered the place from a chair and did as I was told. I rubbed my hands in anticipation of playing some part in the proceedings.

"I'll come get you when we're ready for you," he concluded, and shut the door behind him as he left me there.

I couldn't really blame him for not letting me have run of the place, but after the first hour I started to do just that. I had already given him the names and descriptions of Bartholomew Henry, the shouting painter, and Ed 'Wally' Wallace, the lout. There was no holding back on that, or else I could have just kept the whole thing under my hat. He'd have gotten them from Julia anyhow, and the other girls may have told them to take off somewhere. I could have got to them first, but since I had no authority to make them stay anywhere, I thought it best to let the officials bring them in, which they had. Wally had been found in the room of a boy that was working very hard to dispose of, or at least hide, a "cigarette". The look on his face when the police didn't have time for him was precious. Bartholomew was tracked down in a heated conference with art professor Etchwilde. It was unclear what the dustup was about, but it had begun to get loud. Both the boys came along with little protest. Following behind Scott's crew had been the whole of my involvement in their apprehension.

By hour two, I wanted to kick myself for not trying to do it all myself, or maybe with Dave's help. The truth is, the revelation that one young girl had been murdered and stuck behind a wall made the prospect of a recently misplaced one worrying. If Amanda Carnes was still alive and being held somewhere, I'd rather let the fee go, if the police pressure might find her safe.

After three hours I had read all of Scott's cop plaques twice, and was becoming delirious. An idea occurred to me. Maybe Scott had left something out for me to see. Outside his office, three rows of regulars worked at the desks of homicide and property crimes. The blinds on the office door were down, however, so I moved gingerly around to Scott's chair. I sat and considered if a career in law enforcement proper might be in the cards. Ben's chair was worn out, had arms too low, and looked as though it had at one time been yellow, but was now various shades of brown. Files were piled high at both hands on the desk, with just a window to work between them. Another career passed me by.

I leaned forward in the chair to make sure I couldn't see anybody through the blinds. They were good and tight. I picked the first file off the top of the stack on the right and read over it. Accidental death. Eighty year old tumbled down his stairs. I closed that one and tried another. It was a bunch of the same. After a while, and deciding that Scott did not, in fact, have any treasures hidden there for me, I returned to my designated seat.

By the time the office door swung open again, I had lost hope that the day might come, and so was startled by the prospect of freedom and opportunity.

"You awake, Trait?" Scott asked, standing half in the doorway.

I made a noise that told I was, but didn't jump up, so as not to look too excited. He tilted his head, signaling someone behind him, and came in with Officer Jefferson in tow. He pointed to my chair's partner, and Jefferson settled into it.

"Jefferson," Scott began gruffly. "We need to straighten out this Scudder file. Trait, here, may have some questions, and I want you to answer them. You'd better know the answers too."

Jefferson had been a capable officer in the office, and maybe on a beat, but had only a few months ago been moved up to homicide. With no more than he seemed to have done on the Scudder case, he might have been leaving the streets dangerous to walk. He was a young man, though, maybe twenty-five, with a clean face and neat black hair, and would have other opportunities.

"Tell us what you have on Scudder, Jefferson," Ben commanded.

Jefferson rubbed his hands on his knees and squinted to the corner of the ceiling as he thought.

"Scudder was stabbed to death, at his home, by a person, or persons, unknown."

Jefferson sat up tall, as though ready to receive a commendation for the report.

"Well, Jefferson," Scott acted astonished. "Case closed. Person, or persons, unknown." He looked to me. "Do you know anybody called persons, John?"

"I do not, sir," I plainly stated.

Scott went back to Jefferson, still astonished.

"Me neither. Do you think you could pick this, 'Persons', out of a lineup, if we had him downstairs, Jefferson?"

He started to answer, but Ben boomed at him.

"We need details, Jefferson! What was the murder weapon? Where is the murder weapon? Do you have any idea why? Who are the suspects? You better not tell me Ed Wallace checks out, because Trait's checked his alibi, and now I've got him downstairs in connection with a murder and a disappearance."

Jefferson sputtered for a moment, shrank at the fury that it ignited in his superior's eyes, took a deep breath, and came clean on it all.

"I'm sorry, sir. The Scudder case was one of many I had working. I deemed it the least important, and wasn't as diligent as I should have been." He lowered his eyes in shame, but added, "He was just an old drunk painter, after all."

I admit, I didn't expect it, and it made me jump as much as Jefferson, when Scott's meaty fist slammed down onto his desktop with a loud bang. Jefferson muttered some apologies, but Ben didn't have the stomach to accept them.

"Ask him, Trait," Scott said blandly, washing his hands of it for the time being.

I turned my head to take in Jefferson, and got what I could from him.

The details were light from Jefferson, but I was able to fill them in, having been to Scudder's garage and house. The medical examiner had reported that the stab wounds had been made by a large blade, possibly a butcher's knife. It had not been left at the scene. Scudder had paint on his clothes. Jefferson thought that meant he had worked that day. I pointed out that he could have found out from Templeton, Scudder's helper, and Jefferson said that was a good idea, and that he would ask that in a followup interview tomorrow, or the next day. At that point, Ben looked so sick of him, I started to worry for him. Jefferson had taken the story of Scudder and Wally's fight at face value, and had even received a completely different alibi than the one I got. The bit about the library must have been after some time to be creative, because Jefferson had gotten that Wally, and Ellen Scudder, had been in the woods camping together. That was the bag.

"Out," Scott seethed. Jefferson didn't have to be told twice, and jumped up and left. I stood, stretched, and checked my watch. It was nearly ten.

"What were the stories downstairs?" I probed.

"A lot to look in to. The boys dispute their outings being labeled a cult, but they do say they happen. Wallace is playing dumb, and told us they have them in Lincoln Park, which sounds like a lie. Henry's just strange. We couldn't get a good read on him. He says he experiences 'many things'." Ben propped his elbows on his desk and massaged his temples. He continued. "We're gonna keep them up all night and try them some more in the morning. I've got men checking the park, all the same. It's open."

The last bit answered a knock at the door. The door swung open, under the power of another uniformed man. He addressed me.

"Mr. Trait?" I said I was. "We've picked up a David

DeGrabber. He's downstairs, in holding. Seems to think you can sort him out."

I looked to Ben, who could have been imagining all sorts of discomforts for Dave and I. I pulled some air in, and got to my feet to face this new trial. Ben pushed by me as I got to the office door and waited for the man to lead me.

"I'm going to bed," he grumbled.

CHAPTER NINE

"What's he done this time?" I asked the back of Officer Ritch, as we made our way between the desk rows and down the stairs to booking. It was he who had been sent up for me.

"We caught him vandalizing a wall. He hadn't got very far on it. Honestly, I wish they hadn't bothered to bring him in. I'd be happy to send him with you, just so I don't have to bother booking him."

I figured it was all a misunderstanding, and that Dave must have just been admiring someone else's handiwork while checking the rest of Scudder's book, but as we approached booking a collection of art supplies, bundled on a desk, and a flashlight, said there was more to it.

We went into a corridor with a few cells along one side. They were mostly empty. Ritch called Dave's name as we entered and I saw his mop pop up behind the second barred door. I approached.

"What's going on, Dave?"

His surroundings didn't seem to be harming his spirits. If anything, they were uplifted.

"Ah, John. I've been to more of the locations in the notebook, as well as others given to me by the man that directs Mr. Templeton."

I waved it away.

"Save it. They say you can come out if I claim you. I guess you're ready?"

He narrowed his eyes and frowned at me, presumably for my lack of enthusiasm, but said he was ready. Ritch tried a few keys in the door, which made me glad there wasn't a fire, and finally released Dave. There were some forms to sign, and things to swear to, that I didn't bother to read.

"Don't forget your things, Mr. DeGrabber," Ritch reminded.

Dave motioned like he had forgot, and gathered the supplies from the desk and moved a case on the floor with his toe, for me to grab. It was a sort of box, maybe three feet square, and four inches wide. It stood up on the thin side, and had a plastic handle. It wasn't light, but not encumbering.

The sidewalks were nearly deserted downtown, and cabs looked scarce, so we hauled ourselves, and our loads, over to the L-Train and got on. Dave looked out the carriage window intently as we rose up to the elevated track that gave the trains their name.

"What's in here?" I asked, opening the case.

"They are the combined portfolios of the Loyola drawing students of Mr. Etchwilde," he muttered.

I pulled a still life, in charcoal, from the collection. It was some fruit and other items arranged in a way only useful to art classes. I slid it back in with the rest.

"How did you get these?"

"I arranged to borrow them."

"Uh, huh." I was studying him for a tell, but he never had one. It seemed unlikely, to me, that Etchwilde had allowed all his student's hard work to be taken on a field trip. "How'd you do it with Etchwilde?" I added.

"I had him called to an office for the appraisal of an oil painting." He grinned, almost imperceptibly.

"So what about the flashlight and grease pens?"

"I was trying to trace a work under the cover paint, but didn't have time, or light enough."

It seemed to me like he was getting a little far off from our stabbed painter, or our new case of the missing Amanda Carnes, but Dave always works his own lines, and so far they had proved good. He stared out the window the entire way, even through stops. I reported my scant findings to him, though he made no comments, until we arrived at the station near our office. By then it was too late to work, in my opinion, but it was also the closest station to my apartment, and so we got off.

Sid was long gone, and the lobby was mostly dark. Dave handled the elevator controls to take us up. I unlocked the door and switched on the light, sat the art case by the door, and went to my desk. Behind Dave's desk and chair, directly across from me, usually hangs a painting of a landscape that Dave's grandmother had done. It was at the appraiser's. I chuckled a bit about it. Dave sat at his desk, slid down low in his chair, crossed his arms, and started staring at his typewriter space bar. I watched him for a couple minutes, and then announced that I was going home, and did.

The next day, Wednesday, I made it to the office, not quite as bright and early as I might have. Dave was already there at his desk, with no signs that he had been anywhere else. Same dark blue jacket and slacks. He had no stubble, so I resolved to believe he had slept and showered. I looked over the message pad. It was empty.

"Any word on Templeton?" I inquired.

"None."

"You try the mom again?"

"I did."

The phone rang and interrupted our deep talk. I picked it up.

"David and Trait detective agency. Trait speaking."

"Hello, John. This is Sally. I wanted to talk to you and get an update on my dad. Can you meet me for lunch here in a few minutes?" She sounded upbeat. Upbeat people often have a hard time seeing when they're inconveniencing you.

"It may take me a bit to get to you, Sally. I might as well admit that we're somewhat immobilized here at the minute. I'll have to find a cab, or a train."

She stayed upbeat.

"Oh, that's fine. I'll come pick you up. I'm close by anyhow."

I told her that would be fine and hung up. I sat back

and started to ask Dave if he had anything I didn't, but he spoke before me.

"John, how do you suppose that girl's body came to be behind that block wall?" he wondered.

"Amy Merkle?" I started rhetorically, thinking for a minute about his question. "Well, we know she was made to fit, so less blocks would have to be taken out. If we, for the purposes of this discussion, call her a hundred and some odd pounds of sand, then that'd make a heavy bag to lug."

He nodded slowly as I made the points. "Yes. A large backpack, maybe?"

"Sure. We probably carried them that heavy in France, from time to time."

"Dirt would need to be removed, as well as pieces of the blocks. Tools would have been brought. Possibly hammer and chisel."

"Supplies and body in, and supplies, dirt, and concrete out? Sound's like hard work to me."

"A man's job?"

"Well, murder usually is," I asserted.

Meeting adjourned. Simultaneously, Dave sprung from his chair and began preparations to leave, while Sid buzzed up to say that my ride was waiting downstairs. Dave said he would lock up, so I patted my pockets, found everything in order, and hurried down.

Out front, Sally Scudder waited behind the wheel of a recently washed red convertible. The top was down, though the air at speed was probably still too cool for it. I got in and settled into the clean, white leather passenger seat. She smiled with the wide end of her face, and spoke as we pulled into the midday traffic.

"What do you think? I just picked it up."

The seats had been a giveaway, and now it was certain that the convertible hadn't only just been washed, but just put together.

"It's swell," I told her, as I held my hat for a crosswind. "You having a party?" The back seat, and what little floor board there was, looked like a liquor store, with bottled and cases of beer in paper sacks.

"I just thought I'd get stocked up. We should probably drop it off before we park downtown."

Dave was on the job, looking for big backpacks maybe, so I said I was just along for the ride. She steered us north, and boldly picked us through the traffic to a place I had been. Sara Scudder's house, her mother. We nosed into the drive next to a blue version of the car we were in, and Sally honked the horn twice. Sara appeared in the doorway, animated, and hurried down the stairs. She reached over the door and hugged her daughter.

"Have you been out in yours?" the daughter asked.

"I have!" said the mother, smiling. Her eyes moved to me. "What are you two up to?"

Sally waved it off and explained our visit. I got out and lugged some of the supplies through the doorway, while my chauffeur waited. Goodbyes were said, and we motored back into the heart of the city, and to a downtown restaurant that served big steaks. It would have been well out of my price range, and I even had to say so, but my client insisted on the location, and that she would pay for it. The meal was first rate. My report, on the other hand, was thin. All the same, Sally seemed glad to get it. She paid the substantial bill in cash, out of a new bag with a tag still on it, from a similar wad as she had at our first meeting. It wasn't obviously smaller yet, but would be soon if she kept buying cars, drinks, and tipping double for lunches. I sounded for information on the get-togethers that might have been in the woods, but she didn't have much to say on them, other than that she knew of them. By two, I was back in front of the office, waving a friendly goodbye at the back of her new shiny bumper. I went up.

Dave had returned and met me at the office door.

"Get your hat and coat," he ordered. I turned my hands up at him.

"I'm wearing them, Dave." He was past me, and on the way down the hall toward the elevator. I followed. "Where are we going?"

He wheeled around a step before the elevator, dodged me like I'd jumped into his path, and shot back into the office. He returned instantly with the art students' combined portfolios. I'd called the elevator, and as it rose, he answered.

"Templeton's mother has him at their home. She said she had expected him to contact us."

"She didn't act like it before."

Dave didn't say anything. He only stood impatiently as we were taken back to the ground floor.

I can only figure that Dave had a lot of different ideas at play in his mind, because he got even more impatient when we got to the sidewalk and he started off in the direction of the building garage, where his sedan would have been. I reminded him, not gently, that we were still pedestrians, and raised my arm to try to hail a cab. At that time of day it was no problem, and we got one and were on our way.

This time, I was admitted entrance to the second-floor apartment where the Templeton's lived. The dirty brown carpet of the hallways continued on inside. Mrs. Templeton's aversion to door answering civility must have kept the vacuum man away. Dave and I, he with the large art box in front of him, were sat on a mustard colored couch that would have been just too short to nap on. The lady of the house told us to wait while she went for her son.

Dick Templeton, Roy Scudder's helper, and now replacement, did not instill me with confidence for any job, much less help with a murder case, as he stood gaunt and gangly in an opening of a hallway that led to the rest of the flat. He was all joints. Knees and elbows. They'd even put an extra one in the middle of his extra long neck. You just knew by looking that it would bounce if he were to guffaw, and you knew that he would, under a different circumstance. In this circumstance, however, he was spooked.

Dave handled introductions, and asked that Dick pull up a chair, but he said he'd rather stand, and leaned a bony shoulder into the jamb. Dave started.

"It has been explained to us, Mr. Templeton, that it was you who found Mr. Scudder the morning after his killing?"

"Uh, huh," he offered with a nod.

"Is there anything you can tell us about that? Maybe

something you've had chance to think of, after the time that's passed?"

"Oh, gosh, sir," Dick began earnestly. "You know, it was terrible what happened to Boss. He was a good man, you know. Gave me a chance to work, you know. You know, I wouldn't be where I am now, without all he taught me, you know."

Dave must not have had much planned for that, and moved on to the box he had brought. He flipped the top, and thumbed through as he spoke.

"Mr. Templeton, I understand that you have been hired, many times, to paint over acts of vandalism at locations around the city. I wouldn't expect you to be able to recreate any of the pieces, but possibly, if you could peruse this selection I've brought, you might indicate the ones that are of similar styling. Do you think you could do that?"

Dick Templeton guffawed. I moved some items carefully to the floor, from a table that sat in front of the couch, so Dave could display the pieces.

Dave wasted an entire hour. I don't think I would have bothered to try it, but Dave gave it its due diligence. It was a wash from the beginning. Dick Templeton was no profound art critic. The landscapes, still-lifes, and abstracts, that Dave showed him, might as well have been submarines, birds, and insect repellant cans. Dick didn't really seem to grasp the nature of the game, though Dave explained ideas of form and theme, at least six ways. He was gentle about it, which was probably better than Dick usually got. Dick liked the ones of girls and places. There was one of a desk clock, in charcoal, that he thought was hip. At signs of interest Dave asked if he'd covered anything like it, and Dick would squint and say, "Nah, sir." Half way through, I thought to try to get Dick's take on whether the ones he'd covered had heavy lines or thin lines, or colors or not, but Dave had arrived there too, so I just sat and watched the private showing. The most potentially productive item of the visit was that Dick seemed to warm to us by the end, and promised that he would call the office and let us see the next wall art he covered beforehand. We thanked him, borrowed the phone to call a cab, and left.

In the car, Dave looked downtrodden. Our client had told us that Dick's function had mainly been to just carry the paint, and we had certainly proved that he didn't have much future in using more than one color at a time.

"Sally Scudder is spending her inheritance like she'll get another next week," I reported, to break through the mood. It worked, and Dave tilted his head toward me.

"Really? How do you know?"

"You ask silly questions when you've been disappointed. You know that? I had lunch with her. She's bought herself, and her mother, matching convertibles, and enough booze for one of those college get-togethers; if that's what they're going to be called. It's just Wednesday, too. No telling what her inventory will need to be by the weekend. She knows about the parties too, but isn't spilling it."

Dave looked grim. Less downtrodden, but grim.

"Let's try and find out where the booze is going. She'll want to show off her new things, and the police will release

Henry and Wallace, tired, soon, if they haven't already. They likely won't feel up to revelry after their night of questioning. If she takes us to the spot, we may have less danger of being recognized."

I nodded, but lodged a gripe.

"I've been seen by a good chunk of the Mundelein girls, and I'm unforgettable, but I think we can make it work."

CHAPTER TEN

The rest of the day was uneventful. After a few minutes' consideration at the office, Dave announced that he was going home for the day, and that I should pick him up at his apartment around seven, with Ralph if I could get him. Then we would begin our surveillance of our client.

I hate it when we have to follow the client, for a few reasons. Chiefly, that it makes it hard to trust them from then on. Sally Scudder didn't strike me as the sort of woman that would stab her father to death, face to face, in cold blood, but I couldn't say with certainty that she might not pay some goon to do it. Especially if she knew there was an inheritance coming. Her spending looked guiltless, which counted against her on balance.

As far as things went with our new clients, the Carnes', their missing daughter and these college throw downs were all the threads we had on it. Like I said before, the coincidences that were piling up were not lost on me. Our first client potentially leading us to the best lead we had on our second, and the place where another girl had been before turning up behind a concrete wall, put a question mark on everybody. It was clear that Dave thought he had another lead, maybe in an X marks the spot kind of thing with these covered wall arts. Short of going around and busting the concrete, which would land him in a holding cell that they wouldn't let him out of, even under my watch, I couldn't see how he was going to get to that one.

I toiled the rest of the day, solo, in the office. The floor got swept, and the rug too, as we have no vacuum. The paper and the radio had a little about the exhumation of Amy Merkle. They were spinning it, and fear mongering, to make it sound like she'd just been out for a stroll to a shop, which had taken her by a far out of the way bit of train track, and then had been randomly selected by a boogie man to be entombed in the wall. It was fantastic, but not in a good way. I switched the little radio atop our shared filing cabinet off in disgust.

"Investigative reporting," I sneered to myself.

It was nearly time to go for Dave, so I called the cab station and ordered Ralph again. The operator said she'd send him as soon as he checked in near the top of the hour. That would make me late, but with no wheels of our own, and Ralph the best tailing cabby in the city, it would have to be. He showed up downstairs right at seven and I hurried down, making sure to pocket my .38 for the evening. I got in and gave him Dave's address; a place west, to the edge of the tall buildings, just before you get to single homes.

We were going to be very tardy, and I hoped that college kids did their partying late into the night, even on a Wednesday, which was probably a safe bet, in hindsight. My watch read 7:32 by the time Ralph pulled us under the vestibule in front of Dave's apartment building. I expected to see him waiting impatiently, but he wasn't there. I went in and told the boy at the desk to buzz up to him. He did, and Dave answered, "Send him up."

I didn't want to argue over an intercom, so I went for the elevator and pushed three. I knocked on number 303, twice. A racket came from inside; a banging. It stopped for a second, and I knocked again, and hollered for Dave to come on. The noise didn't start back, and the knob turned. Dave pulled the door open, and I saw what it had been.

Dave's apartment is a good bit larger than mine. Where I have a common room that serves as bedroom, sitting room, and kitchen, his place had all those divided into their own space, like regular people live. Wasted space, most of it, for Dave, as he slept little, cooked none, and seldom used the sitting room for sitting. He had his office chair for that. In this main room he often performed some kind of experiment, that I might not be made privy to, in the working of a case. One such experiment, and I use the term loosely here, was in action now.

The coffee table was flipped up against the bedroom door, with a rug piled in front of it, clearing the floor for action. In the floor were a collection of cinder blocks, in various states of crumbled disassembly, and pales of goop, one of which I believed to be mortar. Leaning against the couch, which was pushed right up against Dave's bookshelf, was a collection of different sized and shaped hammers; from heavy sledge to small rubber mallet. Dave was holding one of the ball peen variety.

"Looks like a chip got you," I informed him, seeing a red scratch under his right eye. "What are you doing?"

It was pretty clear, to me, what he was doing, but it was so crazy I had to make sure he knew. He explained.

"I'm devising a test that we can perform on sites that Mr. Templeton has covered. From what Scott told us, only the faces of the blocks had been replaced over the hole made to fit Miss Merkle, so I've come up with the most likely way that was done, and am now testing how hard such a veneer will need to be struck to reveal it. We can't very well go around bashing all the walls in the city, can we?"

He seemed so proud of himself. It wasn't a bad idea, in principle. My only gripe, which I had no time to share, was that it inferred that there were more bodies to find, and I wasn't trying to think like that.

"We're late, Dave," I told him, showing him my watch, still standing in the doorway.

"Oh, dear." He dropped the hammer to the floor with a thud, and starting beating the dust off his jacket and slacks with his hands. He might have darkened the blue a shade by removing a bit of the grey sediment, but only a shade. He clicked the door lock on, and followed me down the hall to the elevator. We got down and to the cab and went.

With the way the evening began it looked like Ralph would end up with the lion's share of our client's money by the time it was all said and done. Sally hadn't been hard to find, as the red convertible had returned to join her mother's blue one. We waited a fair way off at the curb, and circled the block for a new spot at intervals. Throughout the wait Ralph had asked Dave, sixteen different ways, how it was he had let the sedan go kaput, and Dave gave him sixteen unsatisfactory answers. I was bored stiff by the time things finally got underway, well after nine.

Sally and her mother emerged from the house with paper bags in hand, and loaded them into the red car. Dave tried his spyglass that he keeps in his pocket, but there wasn't enough light. I just made out goodbyes being said, and saw the elder Scudder return to the house. I told Ralph to start the motor, and he did. Dave and I ducked down below the level of the car windows, as Sally Scudder pulled out of the drive and started in our direction. I put a hand on Ralph's elbow to hold him from making a premature u-turn.

"She's turned left at the corner," Dave observed.

I released my grasp, and Ralph spun the car around and followed.

The itinerary was not direct. We poked along, hiding among the evening traffic, for stops at a liquor store, a druggist, and a gas station. More supplies had to be purchased. Finally, she led us back to the Loyola campus, around midnight. She stopped at the corner of Sheridan and flashed her lights. Four females appeared from the darkness and piled into the little convertible, the five of them causing the car to ride low. She was off again, and going north. My eyes were mostly on the convertible, but a sound brought my attention to something else.

On both sides of the street, staying out of the lights, but doing nothing else to conceal their presence, was a scattered exodus of young people. Some lugged sacks, and others wore backpacks. The odd whoop, or holler, told me their burdens were recreational in nature. I told Ralph to fall back and let us out.

"Turn up that side street, please," Dave suggested.

Ralph did as he was told, and we disembarked. The idea now was to infiltrate the migration on foot. The darkness made it easy, and Dave and I fell into the loose ranks. I pulled my hat low to further hide my face. A couple of boys, double teaming something long and heavy, wrapped in a cover, hurried by with their load at a trot. Behind them came another guy with a satchel full of tent poles hoisted over his shoulder.

It was a slow moving procession, and Dave and I were trying not to linger near anybody very long, and so were making our way to the rear by allowing them to overtake us. After what felt like five miles, but may have only been three at the most, due to pace, the swarm left the roadway, and entered a wooded area that I knew to have beach beyond. Dave motioned for he and I to keep walking, and we did for another block, until we could see a path to flank the group into the trees. That's what we did, picking our way carefully and as quietly as possible through the dark canopy. Soon the sound of voices reached us. Not boisterous, but enthusiastic. Now we were taking cover as we came to it, not knowing how close we had come to the meeting. Dave and I moved from tree to tree, scanning ahead with our ears as much as our eyes.

We froze in our tracks at the fairly close sound of someone hammering the tent stakes into the turf. I stepped behind a big tree and beckoned Dave to join me. He did, and peeked around and listened from the left side of the conifer. A small fire was beginning to burn under an open spot in the canopy, illuminating faces around it. Sally Scudder was there gathering her supplies as volunteers brought the bottles to her from out of the darkness beyond. She offered beers freely too. A tent, the square kind that a gypsy might use, was being erected a few feet from the fire by a couple of boys. Someone with a guitar sat on the end of a fire log and strummed and sang pieces of songs, while the boys and girls paired off and danced as they imbibed. We watched for ten minutes there, looking for faces we recognized, or maybe for someone to be ushered off, possibly to their doom.

No doom to see. What I did see, however, was a good bit more skin than I expected for a catholic university. As the night went on, and the fire burned brighter, layers came off. Some of the girls were down to just their underwear, and nearly all the boys had gone shirtless. I don't think myself naive, in fact, I know I'm not. It's just that there's a part of my brain that wants there to be some consistency between my expectations and the reality. On one hand, I know that college aged young men and women are going to do the sort of things that young men and women do, and saying that they belong to a more pious category often doesn't mean much when looked at one or two at a time while they're half naked. There's just a part of me that, for whatever sentimental reason, wishes it did.

We were a good fifty yards from the heart of the festivities, and so had little chance of being seen. The voices had raised as the alcohol supply had dropped, and so I didn't hear the footsteps as they approached my hiding place. A hand grabbed my collar and pulled as I was tackled to the ground from my right. The blow hadn't come fast, but it carried a lot of weight, and I went down. He'd struck me in the ribs, below my arm, so I had it free. I wriggled around to get some leverage. He was on my legs, and it made it hard to reposition. I managed to get something head shaped between my bicep and forearm, set it for a head-lock, and tried to squeeze the skull like I was trying to smash a watermelon. Immediately, as the pressure came on, I heard a muffled cry from a woman. It sounded like it had come from the melon. I twisted hard and freed a leg, looked down and saw long blonde hair, and let go.

"Let go of her," a man whispered. "I didn't see you there."

The voice wasn't instantly familiar, but the going down had been a shock. I released the hold, and the girl tried to sit up on her elbows. One of them dug into the inside of my thigh, and I jerked, causing her to come down on me again. She couldn't get up either, as her legs were covered by the man who had whispered. He was older, and struggled to get himself upright, but finally did, and offered a hand to the woman. He pulled her up, and then she did the same for me.

After so long peering toward the fire, the woods away from it looked completely black for a moment. The man apologized some more, and as he spoke, and my eyes adjusted, I recognized him. It was Steve Cecant, Fred Washington's friend that I had met while they watched the horses. I hadn't paid much attention to him the first time around. He was nothing special to look at. Just a fifty something year old man with extra luggage around the middle. What was a sight, however, was the state of his current accessory that clung to his hip with her arms around him.

The blonde, whose head I'd tried to pop, swayed like a palm in the breeze, clearly lit. Her maroon blouse was nearly fully unbuttoned, and her lipstick was smeared a little across her face. The rest of it had been deposited in some unsightly way on Steve's face. I say unsightly, because Steve Cecant had not brought a woman from an office, or some other concubine, to this rendezvous. This blonde girl couldn't have been more than nineteen years old.

I know my eyes must have got wide. I did a double take, and caught sight of Dave, to my right, now. It had been he who pulled my collar. He had seen the train coming, but failed to pull me off the tracks. I interrogated Cecant in a harsh, hushed tone.

"What do you think you're doing out here?"

He put his finger to his lips and shushed me, which made me want to plug him, but I resisted.

"Quiet down. We don't want Cindy's boyfriend to hear us." They both giggled.

Now I really wanted to plug him.

"Cindy what?" I snapped.

"Washington," she responded, twirling a finger in Cecant's thinning hair.

I gawked again.

"You don't mean you're Fred Washington's daughter?"

She crumpled her face up at me.

"What? Did daddy send you after me? Who the hell is this, Steve?"

He patted her rear end to calm her.

"Easy, darling. I have no idea who this is."

"The hell you don't," I snapped. "Tell me what you have to do with these parties, or I'm going straight to Fred."

That jogged his memory, if it had been slow. He took his hands off the girl, and held them to me to yield.

"Easy there, Mr. Trait. All right. I own this little patch of woods, and I let the kids come and blow off some steam, is all. It's harmless. Isn't it, darling?"

He sounded smooth in the way a used car salesman does when he's got a sucker on the line. John Trait is no sucker. Let that be known. However, I didn't have much I could do but keep an eye on him, and maybe rat him out to his friend. For now, I just tilted my head toward the fire, and they strolled off. I retook my spot on my side of the big tree.

"That's disgusting," I muttered to Dave.

"She's of age," he responded dryly.

I scoffed. "She is, Dave, but not his age. Hello."

I wasn't greeting anybody, and nobody knocked me down, but there was a new program starting around the fire. The tent had been pitched for some time now, and a man in a red colored robe appeared from it. His face was painted gold. He raised his arms over his head, and the firelight showed the robe was unfastened. He, thankfully, had some shorts on that matched the face paint. At his appearance the chatter stopped, and all the revelers gathered around, some sitting and other standing. I turned to Dave, to say something was up, but he wasn't there. I slid to his side of the big tree and caught sight of him as he darted behind a bush, closer to the congregation. I surveyed a moment, waiting to make sure he finished his move without detection, and made the same dash myself. The robed man was talking by the time I arrived at Dave's hip. He spoke in a loud, pleading kind of voice. I'd heard some new age preachers use it before; not my preferred evangelical persona.

"... fire burns brightly tonight, but will, without tending, smolder and die. So, too, will the spirits within us, if they are not sufficiently tended. We tend them not by tired and relegated regimen, but by acts. Glorious, carnal acts. Pleasurable, or painful acts. We fan the celestial flame within us by the acts that will tomorrow leave our bodies broken."

Someone whooped at that, and a break was made for an uncoordinated hear hear. He resumed.

"But broken they oft not stay. No, my children. For in a short time we shall recover, with our fires fed and burning for more fuel, and we shall have it." A wave of an arm brought action from beyond the other side of the tent. He continued as a large artwork was brought out and stood on its end in the firelight.

"Brother Bartholomew has finished another of his works. As usual, he wishes for you all the share in the Holy completion of his representation of the inner fire."

Bart Henry, the loud painter, despite his late hours at police headquarters, was in attendance, and stepped forward.

"Bartholomew calls for you all to leave your mark, in gold, upon this work, so that some of your inner flame may help us all to realize its grandeur."

The robed man gave a nod, and Henry jerked a hand up as a command to someone. Cindy Washington was apparently his helper tonight, and produced a board with some gold paint on it. One after another, the onlookers became participants; dipping fingers into the goop, tasting it on their tongue, and then making their own version of a Bart Henry violent dashing stroke on the canvas. Shouting was optional, and some did and some didn't. The painting, as it had been brought out, was another maybe-angel figure, but it was hard to make out the colors in the light I had to go on.

I'd never seen anything like it. How had some half naked nut convinced that many people, over thirty of them, to listen to all that hooey without laughing at him? Especially after drinking. Had I not had the knowledge that I might have been listening to the ramblings of a kidnapper at best, or a murderer at worst, I would have had a hard time keeping quiet myself. It had been riveting though, and I hadn't noticed that I was now sitting in the bush alone. I spun on my heel, and just caught sight of Dave's long legged frame moving away through the trees. The chatter of the crowd had started back, so I decided it would be safe to run if I stayed down, and caught up to him.

He was walking fast, and I stayed beside him in silence until we were out of earshot of the party.

"Why'd you leave?" I asked.

He looked deadly serious, and sounded even more so.

"We have no time to perfect the experiment. We have to check the walls now."

I stopped.

"Check them for what?" I demanded.

We were nearly to the road, and didn't have to whisper any longer. Dave called back, still walking.

"For Elsa."

I trotted to make the distance and caught back up.

"Who the hell is Elsa?"

"John, is it that you do not observe, or do you not retain? Elsa was Mr. Henry's helper when we first saw him performing his art on the campus grounds. She's been replaced, and she wasn't present tonight."

The revelation had stopped me again, but only for a step. I kicked back to Dave's side and asked, "So Henry's killing his helpers?"

Dave shook his head from side to side.

"We have no way of knowing that. She may have been taken from him by this robed figure, or possibly someone else in their hierarchy that we have no knowledge of."

"She could just be at home under the weather," I motioned.

"We will find out, tonight."

CHAPTER ELEVEN

They say, in all Their supposed omniscience, that we remember the good and forget the bad. It's how women, not long after the ordeal of giving birth, feel like they'd like to try it again. If that seems like an example that a man can't relate to, then try this one; you ever notice a fighter never starts with the time they caught one and were out on their feet? No. They start with how they beat somebody, even if it didn't win them any money. Anyway, I've gotten long winded on a triviality. The reason I bring all that up, is that there wasn't a cab one to be found as we traipsed away from that gathering in the woods by the lakeshore. The distance would have to have been calculated in statue miles, rather than blocks, and even now, some time removed from the events of that case, I can vividly recall how bad by feet hurt by the time that night was said and done. You'll see what I mean.

"I can't believe that Cecant," I fumed, as we marched south bound, back toward the college and the city proper. I was buzzing with frustration about a number of things, and wanted to say so. Dave was deadpan and tried to derail me.

"You told me little of him in your report," he stated.

"That's because he didn't do anything. He was just there, with Washington, playing horses. Washington was the one whose things Roy Scudder destroyed. I never would have thought, old tubby Cecant, would be out in the woods messing with his daughter."

"I expect she and Cecant's relationship was only as lengthy as we witnessed."

I shook my head.

"You're probably right. It's just gross." With that out of the way, I piped up again. "Now, I want to know who that was in the tent, with his face painted. We've got too many damn suspects. You know what I've been thinking? We've got Bart Henry, with all his helpers. Is he offing them? We've got Wally, who would be built to move bodies and concrete, but why? Then there's Cecant, who might be ten kinds of kinked up. Most of that applies to Amanda Carnes, but not exclusively, and gets us no closer to finding her." I took a breath and went on.

"Then, over on Roy Scudder's side of the ledger, we've got the daughter, looking pleased as punch with her money. The mother, also enjoying the money. And maybe the entire first half of my rant, if they're linked by more than just college parties. Can you untangle that ball?"

Dave didn't answer, and I talked some more as we moved, double time, to Dave's apartment. It took us more than two hours to get there, and the middle of the night chill had set in. We only stopped for him to grab the sledge hammer. I was prepared just to witness the destruction, but he gave me the ball peen to carry. Before his apartment door shut, I had a mind to call the cab depot and have them send somebody out, but standing there in the hallway with hammers and the intent to use them at three something in the morning, I decided the fewer witnesses the better. We went.

Another forty-five minute walk east brought us to our first location. Dave let the sledge down from his shoulder and held out his hand. I put the smaller hammer in it. We stood in front of a piece of block wall that made up the foundation for a piece of L-train track. It was concrete colored, and had a slightly fresher area of gray paint; about a four foot blob, the center about chest high. Dave inspected the blocks closely, paying extra attention to the grout, but the light under the track was poor. After no more than a minute, he swung the ball peen into the wall around thigh level. Nothing. He held the tool back toward me, and I took it. Next he tried the sledge. Same place. The blocks cracked, and he removed some pieces. He made a disappointed sound on discovering more block behind, and subsequently, no hiding place. We moved on.

The night went that way until the morning traffic began. Hours into the excursion I'd asked Dave what the plan was, and if there was any itinerary. He led us to the most visible sites first, so that as dawn broke, we had no audience in our search. By the time I peered a weary eye into a dusty breach in another piece of wall, I wasn't hurting for light. We were also garnering funny looks from passing motorists. Behind this last breach, however, was more solid wall. I checked my watch and read 6:12. Time to call it a night, or a day; it had gotten hard to say.

Dave had kept up a breakneck pace all night, and now allowed his exhaustion and frustration to show. He threw both hammers in a dumpster in disgust, and we walked to a main road for a cab. Finding one, it was time to go to the office.

The ride in the cab wasn't long, but having the weight off my feet caused them to burn when I got back on them in front of the office. Dave stormed inside. Sid was outdoors, leaning beside the entryway, having a smoke with fresh air. I bummed one and joined him.

"I've never seen you come in with Dave," he commented.

I borrowed a light, and puffed at Sid's custom smoke.

"We haven't been home," I explained.

Sid started telling a story about how he had stayed up till dawn once, listening to records with a woman. I only know because I'd heard it before. My attention was on the car that had pulled up in front of our building, and the driver who got out. It was professor Etchwilde, the master in oils, looking down his nose as he strode in, and blinking furiously. I took one last mighty pull of my smoke, tossed it into the street, and hurried in after him.

He'd already found the elevator, and the door closed before I could stop it. It started up, so I went for the stairs. I hadn't even thought about Etchwilde in my rant the night before. Maybe he moonlit as a vandal, and killed his students. Possibly, due to a mix of fatigue and delirium, I thought he might have come to stab Dave for taking the student's portfolios. I didn't come up with a better reason, but took the stairs three at a time, just in case. I was on his heel in the hall when he swung our office door open, and marched in.

"Mr. DeGrabber," he shouted, approaching Dave, who had gotten himself settled low into his chair with his arms crossed. "The unbelievable gall of you. This is theft of the highest order. How dare you lure me away to rifle through and take my student's works? Have you any idea the severity of your crime?"

He'd made it to Dave's desk, and had his fingertips on it while he shouted. Dave was unmoved. He merely pointed a lazy finger back toward the door where the art case stood. Etchwilde looked back at it but wasn't done letting us have it.

"You will pay for this to the furthest extent of the law. You will toil in the fields around the strongest prison for this crime against my pupils, and myself."

Dave, displaying not the slightest hint of offense, tilted his head to the professor, and asked,

"You told us Bart Henry was not a student of yours, yet his works are among those of your class. How is that, Mr. Etchwilde?"

It didn't look like Etchwilde would move any furniture around, so I made my way over to my desk, and had his face. It amused me that at the question, his rate of blinking actually increased. I also had to stifle a chuckle at the blank spot on the wall, beyond him, where our office painting should have been. He scoffed three consecutive times, and then deigned us a response down his nose.

"I am made to suffer Mr. Henry in a drawing class that he has elected to take. It is an intermediate study, and I have little say in my role." He scoffed again, I thought in closing, but he piped up for another volley.

I missed the particulars, and Dave probably did too, for not paying attention, because the door needed attending. In the hall, through the frosted glass, it looked like an elderly man in a hat had come to see us. He knocked hard, just as I grabbed the knob. I pulled on it and addressed our visitor.

"Ben, you look terrible," I joshed.

Detective Ben Scott looked even worse for wear than he had the time before. His shoulders slumped, his eyes were redder, and his whiskers, other than his mustache, were unkept. He wasn't down enough to receive my barb without retaliation, however.

"You don't look so fresh yourself, Trait. You gonna let me in?"

"Sure." I swung the door wide. Scott was nearly run down by Etchwilde pushing by me, with the portfolios in hand. The professor shouted back at Dave.

"Every single work had better be here, DeGrabber. Pardon me." He looked Scott up and down after bumping into him. "You're a policeman, aren't you? I want that man arrested for grand larceny. I mean to press the fullest charges our laws offer on the matter."

"I'm homicide. Go tell it to a beat man, or just beat it," Scott told him.

There were more scoffs, but Etchwilde got the idea and huffed down the hallway to the elevator.

"Where's our painting?" I demanded, as he waited for the elevator to come up.

He looked back to me and blinked.

"At the school," he spat, as the doors opened.

Scott went by me, and I shut the door after seeing that Etchwilde was in the elevator and on his way out of our lives, for now.

Ben grabbed his own chair, and sank into it in front of the ends of our desks. I got in mine and did likewise. The three of us sat in silence for a few moments, generally looking sleepy.

"You looked at all those pieces and remember then anyway, don't you?" I asked Dave.

"Of course. I only devised to take them so that I could show them to Templeton. Had I known him a simpleton, I wouldn't have bothered." He swiveled his head a few degrees toward Scott.

"What brings you in, detective? I gather, from the door, that you are no agent of professor Etchwilde."

Ben cleared his throat, but it still sounded croaky when he spoke.

"No. That guy's full of hot air. I've been up all night." His tired eyes shifted between the two of us. "You two have been, too, huh?" He went on without an answer after a shrug. "You know, I told you that finding that girl in that wall had bothered me. The truth is, it's still bothering me, and it was last night too. We talked to those boys, and they gave us next to nothing. The Henry kid is just weird, and Wallace is an idiot."

"I got to thinking about that thing you said, DeGrabber. About the graffiti and the job list. I drove around all night with a hammer in the car, checking a list I got from a guy at the Park District, and any other piece of painted concrete I could find that might have worked for our guy."

He chuckled to himself. He observed,

"I guess I can put together why you two look so beat, and why I kept finding walls that had already been checked."

I admit, I went a little cold at Scott's detection. What with the state of my sleep starved nerves, the broken-down car, and our lack of funds, it would have been the end of us as free men, if he'd decided to arrest us for destruction of city property, right there. He must have seen the fear flash across my eyes, and waved it off with a hand, and went on.

"I don't care about any of that." His tone turned grim. "I found another."

He let it sit a moment, and might have let it rest another, but Dave broke in.

"A gray sculpting clay?" he asked.

Scott turned his hands up with a shocked expression.

"Apartment experiment," I explained.

"Oh. Yeah. The clay held the fronts of the blocks together. The guys at the lab found it yesterday after lunch, and so I didn't have to take as big a hammer as you must have used."

"Where?" Dave again.

"Side road underpass. North edge of EdgeWater. Another painted over spot."

"That's not far from the school," I put in. "Who was it?"

"A less than week old missing person. Amanda Carnes. The one from the paper."

"God, dammit." I cursed, rubbing my tired eyes.

"I know. It was just like the first one. Cut up to fit. They're working out what actually killed her downtown, now. She's fresher than the other one, so it shouldn't take them long." Scott shrugged, and added, "I don't know why I'm even here telling you all this. I guess because you gave me the idea, DeGrabber. Also, I know you guys are only trying to get paid for the dead painter, so maybe I can use what you've got, if there is anything."

If we had anything, then it was Dave's. My head was reeling. So much for the Carnes' fee. So much for there not being more bodies. So much for safe streets. I wanted to find that guy with the painted face and do something to him to make him tell me if he'd done Amanda Carnes, but I couldn't figure what.

Dave wasn't saying anything.

"How does this wall art stuff connect to that Scudder case, anyway?" Scott wondered.

"Dick Templeton is in danger," Dave stated plainly. Scott looked haggard, I probably looked to be in some kind of shock, and yet Dave was still just sitting there, low in his chair, looking straight at his typewriter, with no change in his voice.

"The other painter?" Scott asked.

Dave shot up from his chair.

"Yes. Come, John."

"Where are we going?"

"To question Cecant."

"Who's Cecant?" Scott demanded.

Dave explained as he rifled through a phone book.

"A lead. You have one too, though. Find Dick Templeton, and put a detail on him. I think his predecessor was killed for destroying someone's memorials to their murders. I see no reason why Templeton's work would be received any differently by the killer. Also, since we are now apparently sharing information, contact us as soon as a cause of death is determined. We'll give you what we find as well."

Dave had ushered us all out of our chairs and out the door as he spoke. Scott was either too affected, or too tired to bother with any of his usual, "The CPD doesn't work for you," bit. Instead, he just nodded a few times, told us to let him know as soon as possible, also, and left us to get to his car. It was still super early, and Dave and I had to walk a block east before we found a cab. My feet were such that I was nearly hobbled. He hailed the car, we got in, and Dave gave him an address that he must have found in the book. We were off to find Steve Cecant.

CHAPTER TWELVE

The address we were after took our cab north until we were past the college. Dave and I rode in silence, too tired to talk, and saving what we had for Cecant.

"Stop the car," Dave exclaimed.

We'd turned off the main road, and were going west, and had each been staring out from our sides of the cab. Dave was on the right, and I turned my head to see what it was. I spotted it right away, on the side of an overpass, across the intersection that we were now crossing. Our driver pulled to the curb, and Dave told him to wait for us. We got out and trotted over.

"Is it one from someone in the portfolio?" I asked, as we studied the graffiti before us. It was the right size, and would have taken about a four foot wide circle of paint to cover. Mostly done in white, red, and black spray paint. There were some yellow details done with a brush around the top, as well as finer details of the work.

"It's certainly, 'celestial' enough," I added.

Dave got down on a knee and studied the grout between the concrete blocks carefully. He grunted, and said,

"No one in Etchwilde's drawing class did this. I don't believe there is a body behind it either."

"It's another one of those angels in space kind of things though, like Henry does. It has to be from the same batch."

Dave started back toward the cab, and I followed.

"Bart Henry's lines are much heavier. This is done with a much more even hand. Particularly the face of the figure. Those strokes are even delicate," he explained.

I'm not much of an art critic, so I let it go. We got back in the cab, and told the driver he could continue to our destination. He looked back at us in his mirror like we were crazy to stop and inspect some vandalism. We let him think what he may.

In another mile or so we pulled up at a large white two story place that said Cecant on the mailbox. Dave told the taxi to wait, and that he could probably go ahead and shut the engine off. The driver said, "Suit yourself," and settled in with a morning Tribune.

We got out and climbed the drive. Cecant's place was similar to his friend Washington's. All the house that could fit on the lot. No porch, however. Just a couple of steps leading to a big brown paneled door.

Dave knocked.

And then he knocked again.

One more set of raps, and two looks at my watch, said something was up. I had no good reason, but I just couldn't see Steve Cecant tearing down with the college kids till all hours of a Wednesday night, and then getting to work bright and early at whatever it was he did. I motioned for Dave to follow me around back. Around the drive and the two-car garage, that was built on to the house, we came to a gate on a privacy fence. It was unlocked, so we went in. Construction was in progress in the backyard. A pallet of blocks, and a pile of fill dirt were waiting to be arranged within a layout of string that would be poured as a patio.

"Well, Cindy Washington is still breathing," I observed. I'd spotted her in a second-floor window, but she ducked down before Dave turned to look, so I pointed to the spot.

"Perhaps," Dave figured, "I underestimated the seriousness of her and Mr. Cecant's relationship."

It was as close to a joke as Dave ever got, but the thought was too gross for me to laugh at. We got to the back door, which had some glass in it, and looked in. I'll be damned if Steve Cecant wasn't crouched down, right there, behind a kitchen counter, peeking over it toward the front of the house, presumably waiting us out. I pounded on the door frame, and shouted, "Open up, Cecant!"

He popped up as if he'd been sat on a powder keg. Dashing out of sight, he shouted back,

"You're trespassing, Trait. I'll call the police."

I talked loud, but friendly enough.

"They'd be glad to hear we found you, Steve. Now, open up. We've got some questions."

"I'm not telling you anything."

I shook my head for my own benefit.

"Now, Steve, that's no way to treat an acquaintance.

Maybe I can go get your buddy, Washington, and you'll be more hospitable to him. He'll probably have a question or two about why his daughter spent the night with you." I kept talking loud, to Dave now, so Cecant would hear. "Dave, why don't you run and get Washington while I stay here and make sure nobody sneaks off."

The door latch clicked. I pushed it open, and we entered into a breakfast nook off the kitchen. I looked around for Cecant.

"Now, that's more like-" I found him. Standing in a doorway, beyond the kitchen, looking misused and leveling a pump-action shotgun at us. I raised my hands at the elbows and stayed calm.

"Now, Steve, what are you gonna do with that?" I asked.

"I'm gonna tell you how this is all gonna go, Trait. You, and your friend, are going to leave, and you're going to forget you ever saw me last night, or anyway. Understand?"

I shook my head.

"No, Steve. We're not going to do that. Now what? Are you gonna shoot us both? Maybe you get me, but Dave makes it out the door. You intend to chase him around the neighborhood? I chased him the other night. He's fast. What will the neighbors think? Look, we know your little secret with Miss Washington, up there, and we aren't going to un-know it. What we can do, is trade some of the stuff you know for keeping it under our hats. What do you say to that?"

No sooner than I had it out; a strong proposition, in my opinion, we were under attack. Cindy Washington charged from behind us, and flailed her arms and fists at Dave and I. She came with such force that we were knocked off our spots and toward Cecant. He retreated down a hallway, and we turned to battle the girl. The fists alternated with nails as she made her best impression of a Tasmanian Devil. The melee, though short, brought Dave and I down the hallway as well. I started to find the timing, and the narrower passage affected her range, so I managed to grab hold of a wrist. With it, I spun her around and into what looked like a bedroom. I shoved her hard into it, pulled the door shut, and indicated to Dave to hold the knob. He took it and leaned against her, pulling and bashing at the barrier.

"Dammit, Cecant! Your secret's creeping out from under its hat. Put the gun down and be reasonable!" I commanded.

Cecant had no interest in being reasonable, though. I guess he and Washington were better friends than I'd figured. He was pale in the face, and his hands had started to visibly shake. He muttered something about, "Fred just can't know."

I moved fast. Dave and I were close enough together that I saw he used his moment to cover his ears. Mine weren't so lucky. Lunging forward, I reached for, and got, the barrel of the shotgun just as it went off. I had diverted the shot that Cecant had turned up to deliver to himself. The sound sucked from the room, staggering Cecant and I. He fell back and onto the carpet, leaving the weapon hanging in my hand by the barrel as plaster fell from the ceiling. The whole thing made me sore, and I pushed past

Dave and took myself, and the shotgun, outside to the backyard.

I spent a couple of minutes stewing, swallowing, and cleaning nonexistent wax from my ears, before Dave joined me in the yard, along with a deflated looking Cecant.

"John," Dave said. "Are you all right?"

"What?" I know I shouted it, but hadn't meant to. I lowered my voice. "I'm fine."

Dave nodded and turned to Cecant.

"Who is the leader of the group we saw you with last night?"

"Leader?"

I grabbed Cecant by his crooked collar and backed him up to his wall.

"Cecant, I am not in the mood. Answer the questions."

He held his hands up and looked fearful, so I let him go.

"You mean, Bebotu?"

Dave and I looked from one to another. He'd pronounced it Bee-bo-too, and it meant less than nothing to either of us.

"I don't think there's any Bebotu's in the book. Does he have a real name? Do you know anything about him?" I pleaded impatiently.

"Nah. He's some kind of spiritual character. I don't know who he is, really."

"Does she know?" I asked. Pointing to Cindy Washington, who was standing behind the back door, watching and listening through the glass.

Cecant turned his hands over and raised his shoulders for a, maybe. I got the door, and pulled Cindy out with us.

"What do you know about Bebotu, Cindy? Do you know his real name? Where he lives? Anything like that?" I asked.

"Oh, gosh, mister. I don't know. He's just Bebotu to us."

"Hey, didn't you say he lived in a pool house somewhere?" Cecant had decided to try to help, for some reason.

I put a hand on Cindy's shoulder and gestured with the other.

"Listen, Cindy. I need you to think hard. People's lives may be on the line. Where is that pool house?"

I swear I could see the gears move behind her glossy eyes as she shuffled thoughts around. She hung two gentle hands on my forearm, and leaned her cheek down onto my hand. After a moment she said, "I think the mailbox out front said, Goldstein."

"That's great, Cindy. What part of town were you in?"

"Uhm, it was a big house, in Rogers Park."

"Getting warmer now. I don't guess you've got an address up there, do you?"

She shook her head that she didn't.

"Gerald and Catherine, Goldstein. 3500 Greenleaf," Dave stated.

We all looked at him curiously.

"How do you know?" I asked.

"It's in the book."

I removed my hand from Cindy's shoulder.

"You looked this address up in the book, though? Why do you just have that one in your head?"

"I know the whole book. It's just not worth the effort to recall it, if it isn't necessary."

Even Cecant mouthed a, wow.

I turned back to the couple.

"Listen, Cecant." I can't believe what I uttered. "I need you to lay low here, with Cindy, for the next few days. Get some drinks. Take it easy. No art with Bartholomew. No parties with Bebotu. All right?"

Cindy bristled.

"And why the heck not?"

"Because it's dangerous. Listen, this Bebotu might be a killer. Just stay here, and out of trouble. Can you do that?"

"Hmm, he's a killer all right." Cindy said it like a purr.

We three looked at her, and unanimously dropped it as something us men could never get our heads around.

"Keep her here, and your secret's safe, Cecant," I concluded.

That was all he needed to hear, and lured the girl back inside to have a drink. Dave and I made our way through the yard, and back down the drive to our cab. The radio was on, and our driver was still reading the morning paper, clearly oblivious to the action we'd been a part of. Dave gave the address as we climbed back in. The driver turned the car around and drove us back the way we came. We set eyes on the painting again as we passed it as though it might have changed. It hadn't.

Our next stop wasn't far from where we were. The houses around the Goldstein's were large stone covered estates, with fences, gardening, and little buildings to sit in to relax. The Goldstein's was no exception. Dave had our cab go on a bit past the driveway, before he asked to be let out. This time he sent the driver on to other fares.

"This would be easier at night," I complained.

Dave checked his watch, and said, "At this hour it may as well be the middle of the night for Bebotu."

Fair enough. We approached down the sidewalk, looking for a good spot to hop over the medium fence. We were looking for a pool house, and would need to get around back. Just at the corner of the gated driveway we found a smaller gate, unlatched it carefully, and entered. It opened up to a flagstone path, flanked and partially covered by ferns.

"Looks like our client's going to see us work firsthand," I observed. Sally Scudder's new red convertible was inside the gate, parked in a concreted area for guests. Dave received the message with no comment.

The pool house stood just up around the corner. The pool was an irregular shape, and must have cost a fortune in tile. The path terminated at the tile, with the entrance to the pool house beyond. It had a stone front, like the main house. We abandoned the path, and stuck along the fence as we made our way around. I split my time as we approached, watching the main house and where I was going. In the middle of the day, like that, we couldn't risk lingering too long, and got to the back corner of the pool house pretty quickly. We stepped into a four foot wide path behind, between it and the fence, and got down low to work out our next move.

"Should we risk this window?" I asked, gesturing to a small window high above us. Dave shook his head that we should, so I stood to look. It was too high. Dave saw so, and got on his hands and knees. I took my hat off and put it on his head for the moment, stepped up on him, and peeked my eyes over the sill. I made a sweep of the room and got back down. Dave sat up on his knees, and I retrieved my hat.

"It's a harem in there," I reported. "The kid with the painted face, Sally Scudder, and two other females. Some parts of them are wearing sheets. Do we wait them out?"

"They may all leave at once."

I shrugged.

"If our boss wasn't in there, we could try all kinds of things. She'd out us, though. She might try to kill us, if it turns out she's in on it."

Dave wasn't listening. The wheels were turning. After a moment, they stopped, and he slumped down with his back to the pool house wall.

"What's the plan?" I asked.

He sounded defeated.

"We just have to wait, and hope the girls have engagements to make today."

I cleared a few leaves with my shoe, and took a seat beside my partner.

"At least until Scudder leaves," I added.

It should have all been exciting. A stakeout, right under the nose of a possible triple murderer, but it just wasn't. I blame the sunshine. One of the watch checks I made, before resting my eyes, read 9:22; no hour for a stakeout. Those are meant for the evenings.

"John."

"I'm up." I jerked at Dave's elbow in my flank. The watch read 11:00 now, and there were sounds coming from inside. The girls were leaving. We might have made out the voices and what was said, had the window not been so high, but for now we settled for the stray word and thumping of movement. The door opening around front was clear, and then the chatter did reach us as it bounced over the pool water and off the back of the main house. We had gotten lucky. All three girls were leaving, presumably to catch a ride in the Scudder convertible. Luckier still, all three of them were still in one piece, and hopefully would be staying that way.

We sat tight until we heard the car start up, and then waited some more to be sure. Good thing, too. One of the girls came back to the pool house at a trot, and called for Bebotu to open the front gate for them. He grumbled, but went. Dave sprung to action. He went to the far side of the pool house, and peeked around the corner. Seeing the coast clear, he kept on, down the side, and checked again. Still clear. I was right on his heels in a crouch, as we darted the few feet into the pool house door.

It was mainly one room, with some windows that would have been much less covered, if there had been no permanent resident. The heavy curtains made it dark as a dungeon within. The room held a big canopy bed, a couch, and some wild rugs. Besides that, there were doors to a closet and a bathroom. Dave and I opted for the most direct approach though, and put our backs to the wall on either side of the front door. It wasn't long before the sound of the convertible's engine faded off down the street, and Bebotu returned. The door swung open, and he came in rubbing his head. Dave and I shared a glance and a nod as he stepped just by us, and we took him.

I went for a headlock and made it, covering the mouth, while Dave corralled the arms and hands as they flailed about. I applied some pressure, and the flailing turned way down. Dave explained we were there to talk, and asked if he would cooperate. Bebotu tried to nod, but couldn't, then tried to say something, but couldn't, and finally gave two emphatic thumbs up. I let go, and readied to clock him, should he try to take advantage of our offer. He didn't though.

"What do you want with me?" he asked.

Dave directed him to the couch, and he went. Dave cleared some items out of the way, and sat down on a little table in front of the couch. I stood behind him, got out my pistol, so Bebotu would see, and pulled an ottoman over. Dave got right to business.

CHAPTER THIRTEEN

With only the stray bit of gold paint on his chin, along with some primordial whiskers on his possibly still teenaged face, Bebotu didn't cut the figure you'd expect from some leader of fanatic young people. He wasn't tall, nor was he especially filled out. If not for the tent, the fire, the drinks, and whatever else he found himself in charge of at the parties, you might expect him to have trouble finding any woman, much less three at a time.

"Where is Elsa?" Dave demanded. His tone was stern, but not nasty like mine would have been. I tilted my head at it though. I guess we were looking for Elsa now, without so much as a last name.

The cultist's voice was much smaller without the audience.

"I don't know. Last I saw her, Bart had her for a helper. Did something happen to her?"

"Don't act stupid," I warned. "What's your name anyway? I'm not calling you any damn Bebotu."

"Stanley. Stanley Goldstein. Look, if one of those girls, or Elsa, is supposed to be yours, then I'm sorry. You can have the usual rate, and I'll back off. There's no need to rough me up like this."

I couldn't figure it out. He didn't sound like the nut I had heard the night before in the woods. Even worse, for our purposes, he sounded honest.

"What do you mean, the usual rate?" Dave inquired.

Stanley Goldstein waved a hand like he was relieved, and explained.

"Oh, gosh. It happens all the time. We have a get together, and some girls come over, and then the boyfriends get mad. I try to ask them beforehand if they have any fellas, but they aren't always truthful, see. No disrespect to your ladies, of course."

"We're not here about any ladies of ours," I cut in.

"Well, maybe you two need to fill me in. My father says, always cooperate at gunpoint."

Dave took it.

"We are detectives. He's John Trait, and I am David DeGrabber. We're investigating a number of deaths and disappearances, some of which appear directly connected to your organization."

"Organization?" He scoffed. "Just what sort of operation do you think I'm running?"

"We believe, a cult," Dave told him plainly.

Stanley shook his head.

"Guys, you all are way up the wrong tree. I just do that whole thing for fun."

"Explain."

He sighed, and did.

"I went on a senior trip, with my folks, to the Caribbean, and found a book on spiritualism in a gift shop. It said all kinds of hooey about celestial energies and freeing experiences. Look, my dad's an accountant, and I'll probably be one some day too. All that beatnik stuff is really not my bag, between you and me. It's just that I spouted some of that to a couple college girls, over some drinks one night, and the next thing I know, I've got both of them eating outta my hands. One thing led to another, and I became Bebotu."

I dropped the pistol back in my pocket, folded my arms to get comfortable, and said, "I'm gonna need to hear you weave some of that one thing and another."

The atmosphere was suddenly very casual, and Stanley sank back in his couch, fished for a pack of smokes between the cushions, and offered them around. We all took one, and listened to his story.

"So, the first two girls and I had fun for a little while, but after a month or two they started getting cold feet about the whole thing. I went about it all wrong too. I was bringing them both to family dinners, and out to my parent's friend's parties; like I was going steady with them, you know. People started to talk, and it all kind of fell apart and got embarrassing. That's when my folks sent me out, back here." He chuckled.

"It didn't have the effect they had intended. One guy reached out to me, in another way, and floated the idea of having some get-togethers. His idea was that he'd provide the booze, and I'd try out the heady talk. If I could find a girl for him, then we might keep on with it."

"Plenty of people came out for the free booze, and I laid it on thick. I got three for me, a couple for Bart, and at least one for my benefactor."

"This, benefactor, named Steve Cecant?" I interjected.

Stanley leaned forward and used a tray next to Dave.

"I guess you didn't miss any of the tree branches on the way up. Yeah, Cecant is the guy. Anyway, we added Bart's art to the thing, some face paint, a couple of cheesy rituals, and an exotic name, and now it's taken on a life of its own. The women line up to get in the tent with me. Now, what's all this about murders?"

"We'll get to that." I held him up. "So this whole thing; the parties, the name, the crazy speeches. It's just a ploy to get girls for you and Cecant?"

He turned his hands up.

"Well, sure. I don't believe in any of that celestial energy crap." He laughed at a thought and let us in on it. "Now, Bart. He's a true believer. That guy's a trip. He says all the same stuff to attract a pretty girl to help him with his paintings."

Dave had one.

"Do you worry that any of these girls might take these ideas of free experiences too far?"

"You mean like the ones that left school?"

We nodded.

"I don't see how I have anything to do with that. Everybody makes their own choices, I think. If they want to run off and join a commune, that's on them."

"Do you know an Amy Merkle, Mr. Goldstein?" Dave asked.

"I do. She came to a few of the get-togethers. I think she left town a while back."

"Was she one of Mr. Henry's helpers, as well?"

"You'd have to ask him. I don't want to talk bad about anybody, but she got around to most of us. Wally, mostly."

Dave hopped on that track.

"Did an Amanda Carnes get around Wally as well?"

"She did. Bart, too. I didn't have that one though."

"She wasn't a ball card, Goldstein," I reproached. He cocked an eye at me.

"Why'd you say, wasn't, Mr. Trait?"

Dave told him.

"Amanda Carnes was found dead behind a concrete wall, last night, not far from Loyola, where she had supposedly left. Amy Merkle was found earlier in the week in a similar state. She had been there much longer."

Stanley's jaw dropped, and he let it hang for a minute. He gathered it back up, and asked,

"Do I need to have my folks call me a lawyer?"

Dave's telling of Amanda Carnes' fate, in his matter-of-fact way, had a distancing effect on me. My eyes stared down, looking at nothing in particular, until a form they were on jumped out at me. I reached down beside the couch and picked it up.

"You might yet," I said. Holding a can of spray paint I'd taken from a backpack beside the couch. It had been sticking out of the top of a black satchel of some sort. Dave took the can of white and studied it. I grabbed the pack and looked in.

"Red, black, some more white." I pulled more items out. "Some brushes, and a tube of gold."

I tossed the backpack down, went to the closet, and opened it. I dug around, and in no time, found an all black get up.

"You were the vandal we chased through downtown a couple nights ago," I accused.

Stanley stayed sunk in his couch, and admitted it in a yet smaller voice.

"That was me. I don't know anything about a girl behind a wall though. That's crazy."

"Where's a phone, Goldstein?" I demanded. He pointed to the far side of the bed, and I went to it to call detective Scott.

"Where is Elsa?" Dave asked again.

"I don't know. Last I heard, from Bart, she'd decided to go find her 'true spiritual center'. I tell you, that girl was a true believer too. She's probably off in a berry patch somewhere. She talked too crazy for me, so I didn't spend a whole lot of time with her, and if you say she's dead too, then I tell you I had nothing to do with it."

"What is Elsa's last name?"

"Beltor."

"Ben? It's John. I need you to send a car to 3500 Greenleaf."

"Do you have him?"

"It doesn't feel quite right, but he's worth checking out. Also, put out the dogs on Elsa Beltor." I spelled the name for him.

"Ask if he's found Templeton," Dave suggested.

I did, got an answer, and passed it along.

"He says they haven't, Dave. All right. We're here now. We'll see you when you get here, Ben."

The police came and took Stanley 'Bebotu' Goldstein in, searched the whole place, and charged him with some counts of vandalism, so they could hold him for a little while. Dave and I caught a ride back to the station with Ben, and from there took the L to the office. Stanley was more than willing to cooperate when we left him, which either meant he didn't do it, or worse, was the sort of psycho that had done it, and could go on about his day as if he hadn't.

Back in the office, sat deep in our chairs, and solidly beat, I opined to Dave about our findings.

"What ever happened to just having your one girl you like? Is it kids now, or am I just no fun? Do I sound like I'm a hundred? It's vulgar, is what it is. I don't know, Dave, maybe it's just the changing times. I don't get how so many girls, well to do college girls, would allow themselves to be deflowered, in groups, by that boy. All because he acts like he's got some sort of answers. I mean, he admitted that he doesn't even buy it! Don't get me started on Cecant. That guy. Out there funding and organizing these things so he can be with girls that would be his daughter's age. I hope to

God he doesn't have one either. And he's just getting Gold-stein's, Henry's, and maybe even Wally's leftovers! Disgusting! Do not get me started on him."

Dave was making no effort, whatsoever, to get me started on anything. I only know he heard me because he hears everything. I can't even tell you Dave's position on any of those ideas, because he's never shared them with me. I was indignant, but he likely hadn't bothered a brain cell about it. He just wanted a murderer. Roy Scudder's would have been ideal for business, but any would do now. He and I shared that sentiment. Though I had never met Amanda Carnes, I had been prepared to save her, once her folks parted with their deposit, and now that that was impossible, I looked forward to finding her killer, and bringing him down as the next best thing.

"The Carnes' are here to see you." It was Sid, on the intercom. I pushed the button and told him to send them up.

In a minute we were all four as we had been before. This time the Carnes' said they would hang on to their unnecessary outerwear, and who was I to argue with grieving parents.

"We've come to settle our bill with you, gentlemen," the male Carnes stated.

"You don't owe us anything, Mr. Carnes," I said.

"Nonsense. All the other agencies have had some charges for their troubles. We understand it was on your inspiration, Mr. DeGrabber, that detective Scott was led to our daughter's remains."

Dave put on his most somber tone.

"There will be no charges from us, Mr. Carnes. If you wish, though it would be hard on us, we would be willing to return your deposit to you. We deeply regret not being able to rescue your daughter from whoever it was that did this thing. We are engaged to find him, as it is, potentially professionally, and certainly in a personal capacity."

Carnes let his head tilt down in a great show of emotion.

"That is very gracious of you, Mr. DeGrabber. It sounds as though you will endeavor to earn that money. The police say she had been gone even before we engaged you, I'm afraid. If you could find her killer, and bring him to justice, my wife and I would be very thankful. We want for little, and would reward you handsomely if such a thing may suit you."

The phone rang.

"David and Trait Detective Agency, Trait speaking," I said into my receiver.

"Hey, John. Carl. I just got into that sedan. The motor's toast. You want me to go ahead on a new one?"

Death, taxes, mechanics with bad news. I shrugged, but tried to keep it quiet, since we had company.

"Can you find a junkyard motor, Carl? I'm not sure we could swing a fresh one."

Carl started to answer, but I told him to hang on. An index finger was on my shoulder. I covered the handset, and saw it belonged to Mr. Carnes. He gestured for the phone, and I handed it to him.

"Hello," he began. "This is Archie Carnes. I'd like you

to go ahead with any and all repairs, sir, and send me the bill."

Just like that, Archie Carnes, who I was sure I didn't like, became a lifelong member of the David and Trait club. He gave his information to Carl, and, from my end of it I could hear, Carl sold a few hundred dollars of other services that the old sedan just would have otherwise gone without.

With business finished, Archie handed the phone back to me, and I hung it up. He beckoned his wife to go, and she drug herself from her chair. I walked them to the door, and Archie Carnes parted with a final charge.

"Find that monster, Mr. Trait."

I told him we would, and shut the door. I could have cried, but I like to think the emotions were symptoms of the exhaustion. All the same, I sat in my chair, with my jaw set, and my elbows on my knees, for a whole five minutes before I felt confident to speak.

"You've been thinking. What's the plan, Dave?"

Sat low in his chair, blue jacket on, collar crooked, and arms folded, like I'd seen him so many times before, Dave laid out the plan.

"We find Dick Templeton, again."

This time, I was underwhelmed.

CHAPTER FOURTEEN

For a couple hours I was reinvigorated by the Carnes' show of generosity and confidence. It didn't last, though. Calls were put in to the Park District building, Dick Templeton's mother, and two dozen little manned buildings in the city's many public parks. Nobody had heard from Templeton since he'd checked in for work that morning, but they had all heard about him from different policemen running over the same ground. After a guy at the zoo told me not to call again, though it was my first attempt on him, I gave it up and let the line rest. It didn't even take five, and rang immediately. I picked up again and gave my usual greeting.

"John, it's Sally." Our client sounded panicked. "I've got to see you, now. The police took Bebotu, and think he's a murderer."

I feigned concern and confusion.

"Oh, wow. Who's Bebotu, and where'd you learn that?"

"He's a guy I know. Bart told me about it. The whole school is talking about it now. I'm worried. What can we do? I've got the money, if that's it."

"The money won't come up until they figure out what they think he's done. If it's murder, then the money won't help. Where are you now?"

"I'm at the school, with Wally. We were supposed to go with Bart to work on a painting."

We had a pile of suspects, and I was starting to rate Wally among the top, since he seemed to be in the stable with most of our victims.

"Let's get together, and you can tell me about this Bebotu character. It may be important. Can you get away?"

"I loaned my car to Bart, so I can't go until he gets back with it."

I rubbed my tired eyes.

"Sit tight. I'll get a cab and come get you at the school."

She hemmed and hawed for a minute, but I pressed and got my way. I hung up and gave an outline to Dave.

"I'm gonna take a cab up to Loyola and try to pull our client out of the fire, no matter how bad she thinks she wants to sit in it."

Dave looked up to show he'd heard me, and I left.

I hailed a cab, right out front, got in, and told the driver I'd have an extra five in it if he'd get me there fast. You never know what kind of driver you're going to get. More cabbies than the movies would indicate have no intention of ever doing any hurrying, for any amount of money. This guy here, however, must have just watched a few films where the driver was told to step on it, because he made an inspired drive to the Loyola campus, despite the midday congestion. It was by Divine providence that no pedestrians stepped out into one of the many side streets and alleyways my man used to bypass the gridlock. Arriving at our destination, I handed him fifteen for his trouble, got my feet on the ground, and jogged into the common area to find Sally Scudder.

Class was out, and the bustle of maroon-colored clothes was again on, as it had been on my first visit. Hurrying around the perimeter, I asked a few passerbys, whom I recognized from the forest party, if they'd seen her. The first few said they hadn't, but then one boy pointed me toward the dome-topped science building. I was on the far side of the yard, so I cut right through the middle toward it, and ran right into the broad chest of Ed 'Wally' Wallace.

"Pardon me," I said, sidestepping to go.

He stuck an arm out and moved me back in front of him.

"Cindy Wilson told me you've been snooping around, Trait," he menaced.

I was impressed he'd remembered my name. Admittedly, I was also impressed by the size of him. He looked even bigger with all his clothes on, but just as stupid.

"I've got some work to do, pal." I sidestepped again. This time he waited a tic for me to start walking, before he put himself in front of me, and let me bump him.

"Are we really gonna do this in front of all these people, Wally?" I complained.

In answer, he shoved me with both hands. I didn't

mean to go down, then or at any point, but my feet leaving the ground on his push took the matter out of my hands. Though these were college students all around us, and therefore ostensibly more mature, they took notice of the free entertainment, and formed a circular arena by instinct. Wally held his hands over his head, like he'd won a belt for the push. I sat up on my elbows, and waited for the crowd to settle in before righting myself.

Wally had on a maroon-colored vest that looked three feet wide. I got up and took my jacket off, and handed it and my hat to a bystander. Wally got his shirt sleeves rolled up, and slicked his hair back. He approached with his mitts up at a bounce, moving freely.

They make weight classes for a reason. Ed 'Wally' Wallace was well out of mine. The mismatch was so clear that I was able to make the mental leap right over any idea of boxing him fair. He stepped in for a right jab, and I kicked him as hard as I could in the shin. It got his attention, and the left hand dropped. I stepped forward with the kicking foot onto his foot, and poked him in the eye hard enough to jam my finger. If the next move worked out, the jammed finger might be worst of it.

Unfortunately, it did not. I wanted both hands to go up to the eye, but instead only one did. The other reached out and grabbed my neck. My mind raced through some options, while my hands bashed at his arm and wrist. None looked very good, but I didn't have long to worry about it. He looked real sore about the eye poke, and teed off with a right hand on me. I think he may have pulled me to him with the choking hand, to add to the force he put on my face. I pulled my feet up at the last second, and saved my nose and eyes. The extra weight dropped his target an inch, and his fist pounded into my forehead.

The shock of the blow dislodged me from his grasp, and I was back in the fight. I blinked a couple of times, establishing to myself that I was still conscious, and went back to work. He'd stepped off to rub his eye, and had his back turned.

"There it is," I said to myself with some glee.

I charged forward, got low, and delivered a sweeping kick to the backs of his knees. Some people in the crowd tried to warn him, but he moved too late. He hit his knees with a mighty thud, and supported himself with his hands. This had gone to plan. I'd gotten my leg out before his folded, spun myself around, and sent my knee right for his face. I even managed to get a grip with at least one of my hands on his head, to help with the connection.

"Ooooo...", was the crowds commentary. Wally went back over his shins like a felled oak. One leg popped back out from under him, and he started snoring; the surest signal it was done.

Some Wally fans, of which there had been many, and now were fewer, rushed to revive their fallen gladiator. I strolled over to retrieve my coat, dusted the tail off, and put it on.

"I've got some work to do," I said to the unconscious Wally as I passed.

I had no more battles to fight for the next hundred yards, and pulled the door handle of the science building. A man at a desk was there, and I asked him if he'd seen who I was after. He pointed up the stairs, and said to try the third door on the right. Climbing the stairs felt a little funny, but I held on to the black metal banister, and tried to walk normally.

Entering the room I'd been told to, Sally Scudder greeted me, not flatteringly.

"What's wrong with you?"

I raised my shoulders a bit.

"What'd ya mean?"

"Your head is bright red," she explained, and came closer to inspect it. "Let me get you something cold for it."

We were in a laboratory. The room had, at the front, a big island desk with sinks it, and a blackboard behind, where the professor would stand. The rest of the class had two rows of four smaller stations, made to stand at, that also had sinks. Sally went to a cupboard in the far corner, and opened a little built in freezer. She got out an ice tray, and pulled another drawer for a bag.

"Here, hold that on it," she said, handing me the bag of ice. "What happened?"

"Wally wasn't happy to see me."

She was taken aback.

"And you're still walking around? Did you pay him off?"

"No," I exclaimed. "I knocked him out."

Her mouth hung open for a moment. I reached up and gently closed it.

"Well," she began. "I'm glad you're here. What are we going to do to help Bebotu?"

146

There were stools all around, so I took one, and leaned against one of the stations.

"If the police say he killed somebody, then there's nothing we can do. Who do they think he murdered?"

She leaned on the other end of the station and picked at her nails.

"Bart didn't say. I know he can't be a killer though."

I turned a hand over.

"How do you know? What if they've got him for stabbing your pops?"

She made little fists. I was head shy of fists at the minute, and pulled back a bit.

"I know, for certain, that he didn't kill daddy. I was with him that night, so were some other people."

"In the woods, a few blocks north?"

She sent me a look of shock. I said,

"We do know a little about Bebotu, and the get-togethers. So, one was going on the night your father was killed?"

A wave of rage, or maybe embarrassment, washed over her, followed by dejection. I could handle dejection, because it usually talks better, and she did.

"Yes. There was a party that night. I had been at my dad's to get a couple bottles of liquor for it."

"Who else-"

"Out, Mr. Trait! Out! Out! Out!"

Clandon, the stocky man from administrations, barged through the door, red faced and enraged.

"I should call the police and have you arrested for assaulting one of our students!"

I removed the ice from my head and bristled.

"Assaulted? He started it!"

Clandon pulled on my collar. My argument sounded childish to me, so I let him move me off the stool and out the door. Sally protested, saying I was working for her, and that she'd asked me to come, which the little man ignored. I jerked away in the hall, and told him I knew how to walk. The truth, as was revealed on the stairs, was that I was only just able to. I mumbled to Sally to call for a cab, and she told the downstairs desk man to do it. Ushered out the door, I was met by a mob of Wally fans, who were none too happy with the decision of the fight, even though it had been a win, for me, by knockout. I waved them off, and steadied myself along the science building wall, until I got to the corner and saw the street.

If I could just make it to the street corner, I could sit on that bench and nap, I thought. Sally appeared under my arm after a few steps, and helped me get there.

The report was that I snored, and that she'd recruited the cabby to help get me into the car when he arrived. I received that report at eight o'clock at night, when I finally came to again, on Sara Scudder's couch.

Upon hearing my day's review, I jerked up, lost my ice pack, and kicked over a glass of water on an end table.

"I need to use the phone. Where's the phone? I gotta call Dave."

The elder Scudder, and her daughter, tried to sooth me, and pretty soon I was back to my senses. I got to the phone and called the office. No answer. I tried police headquarters for Ben, and he was out too. In a desperate move, I tried Sid at his house, and got him. He wanted to talk about a poker game, and if I wanted to come play. I said no. He had received no message for me.

Running out of ideas, I put my fist to my head, which smarted. I pushed the switch and dialed the Templeton's number from memory. Someone picked up, and I blurted,

"This is John Trait. I'm looking for David DeGrabber, or the whereabouts of Dick Templeton."

Mrs. Templeton came on, skipping all courtesies, and said,

"He's not here."

I didn't even bother, thanked her, and hung up.

On returning to the sitting room, I became aware that it was more than just the three of us. Over in a corner chair, moving a pencil furiously over a pad, sat Bartholomew Henry. He had one leg over the other, and had on some militant looking black boots with his pant legs tucked into them. The tunic shirt from before had been swapped for a white silk button up with frills down the front. Overall, he looked a bit more like a pirate than an artist. Every couple of seconds his long black hair would fall over his eyes and he'd brush it back. He kept working on the drawing as he addressed me with the same intensity he'd used in his artistic demonstration.

"Did you make any discoveries, exploring the unconscious, Mr. Trait?"

"Nope. Just slept, is all," I said, cheerfully. I smiled at him, and he tilted his head at me. I turned to the women and talked to Sally. "Hey, since I figure your car is back, do you mind running me to the office? I have to track Dave down, and see if he's found Templeton."

Sally looked confused.

"Who's Templeton?"

I mashed my eyes closed at being a dope, and waved it off.

"Don't worry about him. I'm just a little woozy. Can you run me over though?"

She said she would. Sally gathered her things to go, and I checked that all of mine were where they should be. They were, and I headed to the door. Before we got out of the drive, I turned down two glasses of water, a sandwich, and a box of cookies, from her mother, who I at that moment eliminated, officially, from the possible killer pool.

Even though we didn't have a murderer, things had gone fast in this case, and so being out of commission for a half day put me on edge. Sally wasn't poking along either, but she couldn't have gotten me to the office fast enough.

When we pulled up in front of the office, I told her to be safe, and rushed through the door. I looked at the stairs, but they made me aware of how weak my legs felt, so I rode the elevator and leaned on the wall. At my floor, I got in the office. I switched the light on, and Dave wasn't there. It occurred to me that I hadn't thought to try his house, and so I got behind my desk and did that. No answer.

I sat back in my chair, stretched my shaky legs out in front of me, and thought about a nap, just for an instant. With that instant over, I pulled myself up by the desk lip, and gathered the message pad. There was a call from a guy about a dog, a lady that wanted her husband followed, and an owner of a butcher shop that thought he was losing a few pounds of hamburger a month. They all had names and numbers, and dates and times for appointments set. Right between the last two, though, it said,

Templeton found injured. At Cook County ER with police detail. 7:54.

I flipped my wrist over and checked the time. It was only 8:45, so I wasn't as far behind on things as I had feared. I took a deep breath, grabbed the arms of my chair to hoist myself up, and since my chair rolls, promptly fell on my ass.

"Glad nobody saw that," I commented to our little space.

I clambered to my feet, and went.

CHAPTER FIFTEEN

I can only describe the cab ride to the hospital as harrowing. I couldn't figure why the rush, or why my cabby asked, upon arriving in front of the ER entrance, whether I thought I could make it, or not.

"Sure, I can make it," I answered, as I counted out some money for him.

I hurried inside, figuring to find a desk and ask for Templeton's room number, but a parade of police through the place made that unnecessary. There were enough of them to make a dotted line coming and going, so I followed the inward flowing group, and found Dave on a row of chairs in a hallway. He was reading a paper, trying to look calm, but his putting it down and standing to receive me betrayed his act.

"John, where have you been? The authorities found Mr. Templeton an hour ago."

"I took a nap. The message at the office said he was injured. What happened?"

"A man found him in a back alley. He'd been stabbed and was unconscious. The passerby ran to a phone and called the emergency personnel."

As Dave briefed me we moved toward a door. Nurses and policemen were coming in and out, and during swings open we could see a crowd of people around a bed, working feverishly.

"Do they have the guy that found him?" I asked.

Dave said he didn't know, and looked like he had some more, but action from the room interrupted him. The door came open, and police and nurses poured out. Pretty soon the hallway was crowded. In another moment a white-coated doctor came out and addressed the throng.

"Mr. Templeton is going to be fine. I need you all to give him some quiet, and time to rest. Even the police, I'm afraid."

That started a rabble from the uniformed men wanting to know how soon they could question him. The doctor said he wasn't sure, and they would have to wait and see, but that didn't seem good enough.

"Hey! That's enough. If the Doc says we have to wait, then we have to wait." It was Ben Scott, coming from somewhere further down the hall. "Go find something to eat. It's gonna be a long night." The group relaxed and began to go. He added, "And get a couple boxes of doughnuts."

Maybe it was code, or maybe Ben had a particularly nasty disposition without them, but the doughnut request really had an effect on his men, and they took off double time. That left Ben, Dave, the doctor, and myself in the hall; the nurses having moved on immediately to other tasks.

"Well, we found him, DeGrabber," Scott announced.

"What happened to him, Ben?" I asked.

"Sir, do you need medical attention?" It was the doc. He put his hands on my shoulders, spun me toward him, and shined a light in my eyes. "No response," he muttered to himself. "Have you been in some sort of accident, sir?"

I pulled away and stumbled down into one of the chairs on the wall. I like to think it looked natural, but the little turn, and the light, had done my head in. I rubbed it and answered.

"A guy hit me, but I'll be fine in the morning."

"Who hit you?" Ben demanded.

"Ed Wallace."

He turned to Dave.

"Is Wallace still in on this?"

I didn't hear Dave's answer, but I knew it was an affirmative. The doctor was bent down, checking my eyes and pulse. He offered me some aspirin, at least, which I readily accepted. He straightened up and went off to find it.

"Hey!" Ben called down the hallway to one of his men. "Get me Ed Wallace."

I guess the officer said he would. Ben came and took a seat on my right. He shifted around, and put his hat on his knee, revealing his hair, as bright red as the mustache.

"You two have anybody else I should send for?"

Dave answered, leaning on the hallway wall.

"Have you found Elsa Beltor?"

"No."

"What was Mr. Templeton doing in that alleyway?"

"He was working. Paramedics say he had a paint roller and a big bucket of gray there by the wall."

Dave had been leaning, with his arms folded for murder thinking, but on the news jerked straight up and his arms shot down. I'd never seen him so excited.

"Had he already finished?" he blurted.

Ben wasn't putting much of it together, or didn't think it too important. He bobbed his head around, and said,

"I don't know. I'm hoping he'll just tell us who stabbed him. That's what you wanted him for, right? To identify the killer?"

Dave stamped a little circle, like he wanted to run somewhere, but had to stay and talk.

"No. No. No. No," he rattled. "We need him to show us one of the killer's pieces."

"Pieces of what?" Ben was getting sore.

"Of art! Don't you see? The entire city is littered with the work of amateurs, in back alleys and under bridges. A few of these, hopefully very few, mark the locations of someone's victims. The previous ones have been covered when we've found the bodies. If Templeton was stabbed for trying to cover another, then the work may still be intact. An analysis of it will almost certainly lead to our man."

"Oh." Ben let it sit for a moment while it all congealed. "Well, let's just take my car to the spot and look then."

He didn't have to tell Dave twice. He was off down the hallway, stretching his long legs. Ben got up and offered me a hand. I pulled on it, and got to my feet. The doctor came back just then with a little cup. I paused for a moment and swallowed whatever was in it, and rejoined my party.

Ben went to the first squad car he saw, got in, and started it up. Dave got in the passenger side, which put me in the back, with no door handle of my own. I leaned up, and held onto the cage, so I didn't miss any of what was said.

"Have you gotten a cause of death for Amanda Carnes?" Dave inquired.

Ben nodded as he checked his mirror to merge.

"I did. It was bad."

Ben described the thing in detail, but at risk of there someday being children listening, I'll just say that it had all been done with a knife, similar in type to the one that killed Roy Scudder, but with much more time and inventiveness. If you read between the lines, you may get the picture later, but I don't want to spoil that part now.

We only had to get downtown, toward the north end of the loop, but a call came in on the car radio, saying Templeton was up, so we turned around. That threw Dave into a fit and a tirade, but Ben won out, since he was at the wheel. Something about my seat in the back, like a common crook, made me feel like I couldn't have a side on it, but if I'm honest, Ben's idea about Templeton saying who stabbed him, directly, seemed to me like the way to go. A future jury might not all be art critics, after all.

Ben hit the lights and siren as he pulled a u-turn, right there in the middle of Harrison Street. Another blow to my mental faculties. We were back in front of Cook County in no time, the entire excursion lasting maybe ten minutes.

Dave and Ben started to rush inside, but I banged on the glass to remind them I was stuck. They let me out, and we all hurried back to Templeton's room.

The doctor was standing in front of the door, with his hands out, trying to hold four of Ben's men at bay.

"Move out of the way. Out of the way." The gathering did as commanded, and Ben talked to the doctor.

"Doc, we gotta talk to that man, right now, if he's up. There's a murderer on the loose, and he may have just been up close and personal with him."

"I understand, Detective, but Mr. Templeton is very weak right now, and should not be put under any undue strain."

"We'll talk soft," Ben assured, as he slid through the door. Dave was right behind him and made the gap as well. The doctor gave up, deciding the more the merrier, and I put my hands together to apologize for the others as I sidled past too.

Templeton looked pale in the face, and lanky as ever, but from what was exposed you couldn't see anything out of the ordinary. We stood three abreast beside the bed that was laid flat.

The doctor joined us, locked the door, and whispered,

"Mr. Templeton was stabbed in both kidneys from behind."

I was furthest down the line and nodded for all of us.

"Who stabbed you, Templeton?" Scott nearly shouted.

The doctor shushed him furiously. Dave offered a much gentler prompt.

"Tell us what happened, Mr. Templeton. If you're

able. We've been searching for you since very early this morning."

Templeton spoke as clearly as a man could be expected to on the amount of morphine he must have had.

"Oh, gosh. I've been working so hard trying to catch up, you know. Turns out, old Roy had marked some jobs off that he hadn't actually done, so to make it up to the boss, I've been going around and repainting all the spots, whether they needed it or not."

I put my head in my hand. Not another empty interview from the elusive Dick Templeton, I thought.

"This last site you were tending to, was it to be repainted?"

Templeton shook his head, and then winced like he shouldn't have.

"No, sir. It was one Roy hadn't done."

Dave couldn't hide his grimace as he asked the next part.

"Did you cover the entire work, Mr. Templeton?"

Relief fell over us all when he answered.

"I didn't even get started. I drug the stuff around to the spot, you know, cause that alley by the tracks wasn't supposed to be blocked, and was just getting some paint in the tray when I got a hurt. It was bad, mister. I went down, and he got me a couple more times, and ran off. I guess he thought he'd finished me. About did, too, according to doc, here. It was daylight when I went out, you know, and now it's night time out the window here, so I don't know how long I was out there bleedin'."

His composure impressed me. He gave us all that like

he was telling us about wasted paint. Dave followed up with more questions.

"What time did you get to that alley, Mr. Templeton?"

Dick tried to shrug his shoulders, but abandoned it almost immediately.

"I don't know. Like I said, I been trying to catch up, so I've been working as long as there's light. The paint's no good for watches anyway, you know."

Ben had one, and tried to keep his voice down for it.

"Did you happen to get a look at the guy? Did he say anything? Maybe you saw something that stuck out."

"No, sir. He came up from behind. You know, though, after he ran off, I could see up to the next main road. I thought if I could get some strength up, I might could make it there. I even saw a little red fire truck pass by, just before I went out."

Ben stepped out of the line and muttered some things under his breath that you don't need to hear. I had my eyes on Templeton, honestly admiring him for the job he was doing. I'd seen military men, first hand, unable to give a report of a firefight of Templeton's quality, and they hadn't even been hit. Something was bothering him though, and his face seemed not to point to his cut up kidneys, but higher up. A thought was forming, so I tried to help him with it.

"What's on your mind, Dick?" I asked.

He tilted his head, winced, and put it back in the comfy spot.

"Well, it's just that," he thought for another second and

spilled it the best he could. "I've never seen such a little fire truck, you know."

Even my compromised bean was able to make that leap.

"You sure it wasn't a little red convertible, Dick?"

He jerked like he meant to sit up, and instantly regretted it.

"It was a little red convertible. Come to think of it, I think I'd seen it before. Yeah. It followed me around in the truck the whole afternoon."

Dave turned to me.

"What does that mean, John?"

I pulled him around away from the bed, gathered Ben into the huddle, and explained.

"Sally Scudder loaned her new red convertible to Bart Henry this afternoon. That's why I had to go to her earlier. She didn't have her car. That makes Bart Henry it, doesn't it?"

"It's enough to pick him up on," Ben stated, and left the room, presumably to put the bee on Henry.

Dave didn't look convinced.

"She may have done all this herself, or they may all be working in concert."

I shrugged.

"Henry was at her house, when I came to, earlier."

Dave shot me an inquisitive look.

"I'll explain later."

He nodded, and made a suggestion.

"Let's find Detective Scott. His men will have looked

into Henry from when they had him in with Wallace. Maybe some background will assist us."

He went out the door, leaving me and Templeton in the room with the doctor off in a corner. I went over and patted the patient on the wrist, told him thanks a bunch, and followed after my colleagues.

I tried to rush down the hall, the best I could, toward the sound of a gathering. Ben had assembled a group of officers, and was giving them their task.

"... He dresses kind of strange. Flowy shirts, beatnik type."

I piped up.

"Last seen in a white button up, with ruffles down the front, and big black boots with the pants tucked in. He might be driving a new red convertible."

The officers looked at me like I'd stepped off a spaceship.

"You heard him. Go!" Ben ordered.

They shuffled off, breaking up into pairs, and divvying territory. Their absence revealed Dave there, close by. Scott took off toward the exit at a march, and we followed.

"Do you have Bart Henry's background information, Detective?" Dave asked.

"No, but I've got a hammer in my car, and I mean to use it on that wall that Templeton was about to cover."

We followed him out and down the sidewalk to a parking lot. There we boarded Scott's unmarked rig. He fired it up, and peeled out into the night traffic.

The car radio was alight with the chatter of search coordination, as well as the usual calls. The Chicago Police were in their element now. Putting together obtuse puzzles wasn't always their bag, but I had to admit they had something for this known manhunt that Dave and I would never. Manpower.

A few moments of the chatter was all Ben needed to hear to feel good enough, or get bothered enough by it, to shut the set off. Ben's car had a clear bench in the front, save for a medium-sized mallet hammer, so we rode three abreast to the site of Templeton's misfortune. There was still a crew in the alley working the crime scene, and they had it blocked. We parked and got out. The boss marching down the alley and into the crime scene of a little stabbing, with a hammer in hand, had an arresting effect on the men. They stopped what they were doing and looked from one to another, trying to decide who would find out what the hubbub was about.

The big paint bucket and rolling tray were still where Templeton had left them, ready to go on the stain on the side of a blocked embankment that supported a piece of L-train track.

Dave didn't need but a glance. He turned around to go back to the car. Honestly, I could see it plainly too. The low light of the alley didn't make it difficult, because I had seen Bart Henry paintings in both the day and the night. This was clearly another one of them. Ben went to it.

"Hey!" He called to one of his guys. "Come take a picture of this."

A man with a camera did as he was told, taking two exposures to be sure he had it.

"You got it?" Ben confirmed. The man nodded, and Ben laid the hammer into the bottom portion of the painting with a hard swing. Some chips of concrete flew up, and he brought the hammer to bear a second time. More pieces. Another three strikes seemed like enough, and he picked the pieces away and felt into the hole he'd made.

"What the hell?" he exclaimed.

I came closer.

"What is it?"

"There's nothing here."

"What?"

"DeGrabber!" Ben shouted.

Dave was leaning on the car hood at the end of the alleyway, paying no mind.

Ben shouted again, this time booming, causing Dave to jump. He looked up at the sky in frustration, and made his way leisurely back to us.

"What more do you need to see?" he asked impatiently.

Ben pointed with the hammer handle down to the hole in the blocks, and explained.

"No body, DeGrabber."

Dave's eyebrows went up, and he dropped to a knee to inspect the lack of findings. He folded his arms there, and stared at it for at least a whole minute. Ben and I waited for something to happen. We nearly jumped when Dave suddenly offered some speculation.

"Could it be that Bartholomew Henry is deteriorating? Which was worse, detective?"

"Which what was worse, DeGrabber? And what about Henry?"

Dave stood.

"Amy Merkle, or Amanda Carnes. Which was worse? Which showed the signs of the most suffering?"

"Amanda Carnes, probably. The ME said Merkle was killed, then cut up, whereas Carnes had it all done at once."

I winced at the thought.

Ben shared an issue he had.

"DeGrabber, with no body here, are we even sure those girls behind the walls have anything to do with the two stabbed painters?"

Dave had stepped off to think some more, and now turned back to Ben and I with a look of disgust.

"Of course they do, detective. You described Henry's gruesomeness to us just a little while ago."

Ben was out of patience with Dave. He dropped the hammer, stepped to Dave, took him by the collar, and pushed him into the wall against the painting.

"What does that have to do with Templeton in this alley, DeGrabber?" he shouted.

Dave, ever composed, took no offense to the rough handling. He lifted a finger above his head, and pointed to the artwork.

"That, is a depiction of Saint Bartholomew, who is said to have been flayed and beheaded for his part in converting the brother of an Armenian king. The true particulars of his martyrdom are somewhat conflicting, but the legend works quite fittingly with Mr. Henry's flair for the dramatic. Wouldn't you say?"

Ben released him and looked up at the mural. It was good enough to be called that. I guess the only difference between a mural and graffiti is somebody's say so. I'd heard that thing about Saint Bartholomew, but had never put the story together with his popular depiction as a guy who was peeled like a banana. There it was, though. Bigger than the other ones would have been. This one would have taken at least an eight foot blob of gray to cover. Saint Bartholomew for a new age, with long black hair and a slight frame, wrapped in a ribbon of his own hide. Of course the background was some celestial field, because, like Bebotu said, Bart Henry is a true believer.

CHAPTER SIXTEEN

"Do you think Sally Scudder is in on it, or knows about him?" Scott wondered.

We were speeding toward Sara Scudder's place, hoping to find Bart Henry still there.

I shrugged from the window seat of the squad car.

"Tough to say. She said she was supposed to help him with a painting earlier in the afternoon, but whether that meant poke Templeton with something sharp, or tote paint cans, I couldn't tell you."

Scott picked up the radio transmitter and called for our client to be added to the APB list. It was getting to be a long one.

Scott shut the lights and siren down as we turned onto the Scudder's street.

"All right," Ben began begrudgingly. "I know we've done it before, but I hereby deputize the two of you, yada yada. You swear, and all that?" We said we did. "Are you both armed?"

"We are," we answered in unison.

"This is the house," I announced.

Scott pulled the car to the curb by the mailbox, and we got out. A couple of bad signs presented themselves before we even started for the door, and I pointed them out.

"The cars are gone."

"What's the other one?" Scott asked.

"Blue convertible, same make and model as the red one."

Scott got on the radio again, and had it added to the list as well.

Receiving the affirmative, he and I joined Dave's side. He was already up at the door. Scott drew his revolver, and so I did likewise. Dave was peering through the window, trying to see through a piece of curtain. I slapped his elbow with the side of my piece. He got the picture and drew his little .32 automatic.

Scott looked to us, one to another, nodded, and rapped upon the door the way police do.

"This is the police! Open the door!" he commanded.

No response.

We stood for a second, and Dave jumped off the porch and went around the side of the house, presumably to watch the back.

Scott gave the order again, and again received no response.

"Nobody home?" I wondered aloud.

"I'm happy to be sure. Hmmmf!"

I hopped back as Scott kicked the door in. He'd hardly given any warning, and without so much as a lean backward to gather, he had it hanging loose by the top hinge. We entered.

The phone I had used was dangling from the wall, which gave me a bad feeling. Scott turned the corner in front of me into the living room.

"Oh, God!"

I ran into the back of him as he held up.

"DeGrabber, I nearly shot you!"

Dave was already in the house. He didn't so much apologize for the scare, as much as said,

"The back door was unlocked," and left it at that.

"This is bad," I observed.

The loose phone had been the least of the marks of struggle in the house. The tables were disturbed, the chairs displaced, and the tv and radio smashed. Dave knelt down in the corner, by the chair where Henry had been. It was on its side. He inspected something on one of the stubby legs. He picked at the leg, and rubbed what he'd got between his thumb and finger. Scott left us and started searching the house. I went to Dave to see what he had.

"Whatcha got?"

"Blood, I believe."

"He's got them both." I was grim.

Dave stood, and returned his pistol to his pocket. He scanned the room, and said thoughtfully,

"He may not. A man can only drive one car."

"If Sally's in on it she could have driven the other. That puts her trying to kill her mother though, and I don't like that one bit."

Scott rushed back into the room.

"The rest of the house is clean. He took them straight out of here."

"We were just trying to work that out, Ben."

Ben shook his head.

"Nothing to work out. Come on." He motioned for us to follow, and led us back out to the car as he spoke.

"You guys get too worried about figuring it out. Whether Henry's got the women, or whether one of the women, or somebody else, helped, doesn't matter to us right now. Henry's doing the killing, and those kinds of freaks don't like to share that part. If we find him, we'll find the whole gang."

We loaded up in the car again, and Scott got on the radio to send a team to the house to tape it off and run the procedures on it. He turned the lights and sirens back on, and peeled off.

"What did you mean, back at the alley, about Henry deteriorating, DeGrabber?" Ben asked as he weaved through the yielding traffic.

Dave was in the middle, and put his hands on the dash to steady himself. He explained calmly, despite the jostling.

"Henry has begun to kill more frequently, with less organization. The ritual he used for Amy Merkle wasn't the same after he stabbed Roy Scudder. With Amanda Carnes the method was much more violent, and he was happy tonight to just stab Templeton outright and leave him."

Dave seemed like he had all the answers, so I asked for one.

"Why the painting with no body behind it?"

Dave tilted his head and offered a guess.

"Possibly he meant to just stab his next victim there in front of it, like he did. It may have been Cindy Wilson, Sally Scudder, her mother, who knows. That's what I mean, I fear he's become irrational."

Scott piped up.

"DeGrabber, he's got three murders on him, that we know about, and one attempted. I'd say he's been irrational for some time."

"Where are we going, Ben?" I shouted over the wail of the siren and the car engine.

"Back to headquarters. I've got the men looking out here. We can keep track of their progress, and look at Henry's file. Hold on, there's a ramp here."

Had he not warned me, I would have thought the wheels had come off the car. Scott knew the city streets well, and apparently knew them at speeds that the public weren't allowed to reach. My stomach went up into my throat, and the car lurched as it unweighted itself. I saw sparks in the side mirror as the suspension bottomed out on the way back down. A couple more wild turns brought us to the back of CPD headquarters. Scott pulled into the lot, and we got out and hurried in.

"Stevens, get me that file on Bartholomew Henry," Ben shouted at the desk man. The headquarters were on high alert, and all the chatter coming from the radio behind the main desk was about the manhunt for Henry.

In no time Stevens returned, with a folder in hand. Scott knocked some half empty paper cups off into the floor, and spread the file's contents on the counter. We all three grabbed a sheet and started reading.

"Says here, this is his second year attending Loyola," I observed. "Hopefully that means he hasn't been on the hunt very long."

Dave commented as he read.

"He likely began when Goldstein did."

"Hey!" Scott was barking orders again. "Get Goldstein ready to answer some questions."

A man said he would, and trotted off down to holding.

"Hello," Dave muttered to himself. Neither Ben nor I missed it. We moved around and looked over his shoulders.

"What do you got, DeGrabber?"

Dave passed the page to Ben and shared his findings.

"One of your men contacted Mr. Henry's parents. When asked about strange behavior they said little, but your man suspected more. He called again, getting the father alone, who said that the family have little contact with their son because he unnerves them. The father cites an instance with a dog."

Scott took over, reading from the report.

"Subject cut the dog up after it died. The parents said the boy might have thought that's how bacon was made." Scott held the sheet out with a sour look on his face. "That's gross. How does it help, though?"

Dave pointed to a spot on the page, and said,

"He used the father's butchery."

Scott's hands flashed over the other pages.

"Stevens, get me an address for the butcher shop in this report."

I pulled on Scott's elbow and led him after Dave. He already had his long strides aimed for the parking lot.

"What's going on?" Scott demanded.

"We've already got the address. The dad called the office wanting us to look into some theft."

Scott gawked, but kept following.

"The same one? Are you sure?"

"Henry Meats. North end of the loop. Can't be more than one. I bet Henry, or an accomplice, has been stealing stuff for those parties."

That was all the convincing Scott needed. He picked up his pace, overtook Dave, and had the car started by the time we got to the passenger door handle. Dave gave the address, a corner just up from the river, and we sped off with lights and sirens. The engine strained, and the siren's echos off the tall buildings made my head hurt again, but I told myself I'd ignore it for the rest of the night. Scott got on the radio once more, and tried to find some cars to rendezvous with us, but the big search net had the city's resources spread far and wide, and twenty or thirty minutes is what it looked like. I caught a glimpse of Dave as we passed under a street lamp. He looked haggard from lack of sleep.

The absence of backup didn't bother me too much. The way I had it figured, we were going to face Bart Henry, and two hostages. Possibly, Henry and one of the women were in on it together, but I wouldn't put money on it. The very worst it could be, would be to have Henry and Wally against us, but even then, I'd just bested Wally in a fist fight, and I felt even better about my odds in a gunfight.

What with how bullets don't care much about weight classes.

"Pull into the alleyway," Dave directed.

Scott shut the lights and sirens off, and eased the car down the passage. Henry Meats was right on the corner of the block, and an L train line ran out front. One was going by now, making racket, as we unloaded from the car.

"Blue convertible," I observed.

Sara Scudder's newly gifted car was parked cockeyed in the alleyway, with the lights on and the driver's side door opened. We drew our weapons and approached the vehicle. I went first, with Ben at my hip, leaving Dave and his automatic to cover us.

"We got a body in the car," I informed my squad mates.

Ben went to the front of the car, and looked around it and the alley. I checked the occupant. It was Sara Scudder, and as I reached in to check for a vital, she moaned and shifted in her seat. I was relieved she was still more than a body. I rocked her head by the narrow temples and tried to get her up. She started to really stir, so I pulled my hand away and saw there was blood on it. She had been struck with something.

"Sally. Sally." She started to come to, mumbling, and then clawed at me, and said, "I've got to get in there and get Sally."

I gathered her hands. Her arms were wet noodles. I asked her what happened. She pressed on her eyes and explained.

"Not long after Sally got back from taking you home, I went back to the kitchen to get a drink, and when I came back into the room, Bart was telling Sally to go to the car. He was standing over her with a knife. I asked what was going on, and he hit me with the end of it. I went back at him, and Sally tried too, but he knocked me down, and made her go. I stayed down to make him think I was out, and then followed him here. I guess he hit me harder than I thought."

"Why didn't you call the police?" That was Scott.

I frowned and answered for her.

"She was knocked silly." Back to Sara. "You sit tight. We're gonna get this all taken care of. Some police will show up here before too long. When they get here, just hold your hands out the window and do what they say."

"John, open this," Dave said, standing by the meat shop's back door. I patted Sara on the shoulder, and went to him. He handed me the pick set, and I got to work on it. Scott walked up and joined us.

"The red convertible is further down, parked off to the side."

"Unattended?" Dave asked.

"Looked like it. Should we just kick the door in?"

I was working fast, and let Dave answer for us.

"No. John can open it quietly. We might be able to use the element of surprise. If Henry has devolved he may try to kill Miss Scudder, should we startle him."

"If he hasn't already," Scott commented grimly.

"I got it."

The lock surrendered, and the handle turned. I held it and passed the picks back to Dave. He deftly stowed them away, inhaled, and nodded for me to open it. I eased the door inward, and we crept inside.

The lights were off, and it was very dark. I held the door open as Ben and Dave moved forward. They moved cautiously through a little channel. It looked to be used for storing packaging and paper, mostly. Some light from the street out front shown through a long narrow opening, where things could be passed from the back to the storefront.

Dave's hand went up high, signaling me to follow. The door was on a spring, so I made sure it didn't slam, and moved up. I expected it to put us in near total darkness, but there was a source of light inside that Dave had seen. It came from a crack in a heavy door to our right.

"The freezer," I whispered, as we grouped up to deal with the next entry.

"Also the cutting room," Dave added.

"We kick this one." Ben's suggestion was more of an order, and that was fine, because he was right. By the distances I could get a feel for, the cold room seemed like it'd be large, but we couldn't take the chance of letting our man have a jump on us, in case he was there by the door. We all shared agreeing looks, and Ben stepped back to send the door flying opened.

"Wait," Dave hissed, clamping a hand on Ben's shoulder.

Ben turned to say something, but Dave held his finger to his lips. He tilted his head toward the cold room. We stood dead still and listened.

I could just make out the assertive speech of Bartholomew Henry.

"It's about experiences, Sally. I've found no greater expansion of my spirit than with you all. The carving is my muse, you see." He scoffed, maybe at himself, and continued to preach. "Truly, it is all of you that gain the most from this. I only remain here, though more inspired daily to attempt to capture what you will soon experience, but it is you who will join your sisters among the galaxy's energies."

Sally Scudder sounded strange, but not panicked. I gathered that she had been attempting to bargain, or at least to find some closure or understanding.

"Bart, I just don't see why you've picked me. I haven't helped you with any of the paintings yet. Don't you think I should experience that first, like the others? I mean, even that man you told me about had something to do with the painting, in a way. That's why you chose him, right?"

"Templeton," Scott speculated in a whisper. We kept listening.

"You know, Sally, I had thought that this was the end of a journey. The final coming of one between lovers and apprentice, and master. But then I went to your father that night. I discovered there, among the boring and mundane trappings of his trade, only in the most elemental ways convergent to my own inspired divinations-"

"What does that even mean, Bart?" Sally cut in.

Bart made a sort of growl, and put it into less obnoxious words.

"I mean, Sally Scudder, that your father was just a

painter. He, a lowly blotter, and I, a conduit through the paint with God."

The sound of his voice changed a bit. It got softer, so he must have turned away from the door. I dared to ease it open, got down low, and looked in through the crack. I couldn't see him, or Sally, for all the frozen quarters that hung from the ceiling, but I heard him finish his thought.

"There in that garage, with your father, I discovered that the energies could be gathered, not by the sowing and reaping exclusively, but rather they could come at any time. I learned that as long as I am the one to release the energies into the cosmos, that I receive my share, like extra pollen may stick to the bee."

"Or like the blood in a leech," Sally spat.

While Henry had talked about energies and bees, the three of us had ventured into the cooler, and took up a position behind a crate and between a couple halves of beef. Henry made the growling sound again, and spoke like he was annoyed.

"I believe it is time to harvest what we have sown here today," he said.

I could just see the top of his head now as I peeked around the end of the crate. They were set up in the far corner, but with all the counters, saws, and animal products, I couldn't get my eyes on Sally.

"Drop the knife and put your hands where I can see them, Henry!" Scott shouted, leaving our blind. I popped up, and Dave did too. Scott moved forward, weaving through the obstacles. Henry shuffled around, and had himself behind Sally in the corner by the time I got my eyes and gun on him.

"You must let Miss Scudder go, Bartholomew," Dave said calmly. "There is no avenue of escape, I'm afraid." He settled his .32 sights on Henry.

He didn't have a shot to feel good about though. None of us did. Henry was knelt down, with a big knife at our client's throat. If that sounds like a strange way to get to a throat, then wait till I tell you the rest of the arrangement. Bart Henry had strung her up by her feet, so she was attached with rope to a track on the ceiling for moving the meat around. He had a bucket set up below her to catch what he planned to get out of her, and he had tied her arms to a wooden staff, or maybe a broom handle, so she looked like an upside down crucifix. The arms out to the sides is what made the shot testy.

Ben moved to try to flank him, but Henry scooted around, moving Sally along the track, and got her between us. I looked up and made an observation.

"That track won't let you back her up to the door, Henry. If you try to run out, we've got you. Now, let the girl go."

He flipped his hair back with his non-knife hand, and spoke to us.

"I will spill her blood and leave."

I shook my head.

"One of us will shoot you, just the same."

He sold the idea some more.

"I'll make it so that she dies. I do know I can."

Dave tried another angle. He lowered his weapon, and made his way over to a counter as he spoke.

"Bartholomew, I wish to offer you an alternative experience." Henry's right eyebrow raised, and then they both popped up when Dave selected a blade from the counter he was looking at.

"What is your offer?" he demanded.

Dave turned back to our man.

"I've witnessed your work, first hand. Not in the medium of flesh, but that of canvas. The broad, brave, slashing strokes with which you paint. These bodies, too, are another canvas. A canvas that talks, that reacts without the predictability of the painted sort. Perhaps it is that response that conveys the energies to you."

"What the hell are you talking about, DeGrabber?" Ben stammered.

Dave paid him no mind, and silenced him with a finger. He talked more to Henry.

"Bartholomew, I believe the energy that may seep from two engaged in a work, may be, like the collaborations of you and your apprentices, the most powerful of all. It would be the congruence of all of our spirit's experiences." Dave raised his arms out to both sides, and let the knife rest lazily in his right hand. "Would you accept a collaboration upon our canvases?"

Henry worked his way off from us as Dave made his speech. It was strange, and had held Ben. I figured Dave had a plan, because I know him better, but to challenge the guy to a knife fight, which is what it sounded like he was doing, seemed reckless.

Henry considered for a moment, and stood up. Again, there was no shot that put Sally out of harm's way. He peeked around her ankles, and said,

"I believe it shall be a glorious work, Mr. DeGrabber. I accept your offer. Here, behind the girl, please."

Dave didn't waste any time answering. He stepped quickly around Ben and I, and stood facing Henry, just behind Sally. With the knife off of her throat, she struggled and shouted,

"Get me down! Get me down! He killed my dad!"

"We know, Sally. Just hold tight," I told her. I didn't even look at her though, as my eyes, and Ben's, were fixed on the two men behind her.

Dave pivoted and drove his knife into a side of pork at his right. It was only a violent action because the blade went in down to the handle, but Dave had done it so casually that Henry hadn't felt threatened. He pulled the knife back and spoke, just as calmly.

"Are you ready, Mr. Henry?"

"I am," he answered.

Dave settled his shoulders, and leveled his eyes on his man. Henry thrusted forward, just as Dave had into the pig. Dave turned to dodge, and made a move that I had no time to admire then, but will never forget. With his left, he took Henry's wrist and pulled him forward, and with his right he brought the knife up and slashed the rope that held Sally's feet to the track. She yelped as she crashed to the floor in an awkward heap. By the time her feet found the floor the two men had switched sides, and Henry was a good two strides clear of Sally, and maybe five feet from

Dave. Dave turned his head to Ben and I, and commanded, just as calmly as he had been,

"Fire."

We didn't have to be told twice either. I think I was the first on the trigger, but we were both on target, opening up on Bartholomew Henry like a chilly firing squad. He twisted as our .38's fell into him, and went down dead on the spot after the sixth or seventh. Sally screamed, surprised by the noise I guess, and clambered to a seated position just as Henry's head hit the cold floor. Dave knelt down and cut the broom handle off of her. He offered a hand and got her up.

"He's gone," Ben announced, removing his fingers from Henry's neck. He re-holstered his pistol, and stood looking at the body with his hands on his hips. I got my gun put away as well, patted him on the shoulder, and followed Dave out of the freezer; he was leading our client by the arm, as the hanging had messed with her legs and balance. By the time she made the back alley she'd found her legs enough to go to her mother.

CHAPTER SEVENTEEN

The time I should have been in the office the next day be damned. By the time I returned to consciousness that morning, it turned out to be one o'clock in the afternoon. Even after sleeping the night away, with no alarm, I was dragging as I got myself ready for a day off. The events of the Scudder case, and all that, seemed like they'd taken a month's worth of energy. The morning paper, that I took late, had news, to me, in the upper corner, that it was only Friday. There was stuff in there about the case too. We let Scott put the official spin on it, which painted us somewhat as bystanders, but that was always the deal, so we could maintain our working relationship, and everyone's dignity. With Dave being the hero this time, and deputized, there was a little shine left for the David and Trait Agency.

The extra police had arrived to the meat shop just a few minutes after Henry hit the floor, and had a million questions for all three of us. To Ben's credit, he pushed his men off of us as if we were one of his own. With the way my head felt, and as weary as Dave and I were, we'll be eternally grateful for him not keeping us up till dawn.

At four o'clock, Ben, Dave, and I found ourselves around a corner table at Joe's Bar. It was the first quiet dive you could find near the Police station. Ben had the floor.

"I took the day off, but went in to get an update. We worked Goldstein over, and he's as good as out of it. Rounded up Wallace, too. He wasn't very forthcoming until we put him and Goldstein on ice in the same cell. Once Goldstein told him the jig was up, and that there had been murder involved, he was happy to help. We searched his place, and even Ellen Scudder's house, and they weren't involved in the killings either."

"What about Steve Cecant? He was supposed to have been watching that Wilson girl," I wondered.

"We went and got him. He was at his house, like you said. He'd lost track of her, but we got her at the school. You know, for the sort of creep he is, and Goldstein too for that matter, the both of them were staggered by what Henry had done. Cecant says the girls aren't worth it to him, if that kind of thing might come along with it, so he's not going to be having anymore get-togethers."

"And Goldstein?" Dave probed.

"Swears to retire his faux spiritual act, at least in a public capacity. He was very cooperative. I feel as good as I can about him."

I took a sip of my drink, a gin and tonic. My friends did the same. Setting the glass down, I asked,

"How about that girl?"

"Elsa Beltor," Dave clarified.

Ben exhaled, disturbing his mustache hairs. He shook his head as he explained.

"We're busting blocks out of every wall that Scudder, or Templeton, painted in the last two years. So far we haven't found any presents. We even checked Goldstein's spray paint spots first, before we let him go, just to be sure. Near as I can tell, she's disappeared, or was disposed of some other way. We're keeping the file open though."

"That's good," I said. I looked up and thought a little prayer for her.

Ben put his glass down, and wiped at his mustache. He cut his eyes at Dave, crossed his arms, and asked a question.

"DeGrabber, I want to know how you figured you wouldn't get stabbed back there in the meat locker?"

Dave made only the slightest grin, erased it, and answered.

"I knew what his attack would be."

Ben turned a hand over.

"How the hell did you know that?"

Dave explained.

"I made him use the low forward thrust. I planted the move when I made it on the side of pork."

"How could you know he'd do the same as you, DeGrabber?"

Dave uncrossed his arms and pointed a finger at the both of us.

"I've made the two of you cross your arms, just now."

Ben and I were suddenly aware that we were indeed doing our own impersonations of Dave's usual position. I could see Ben didn't buy it, but he was conflicted because he had seen it for himself. I piped up, so he didn't have to wrestle with whether Dave was pulling his leg. Neither of us would have ever figured that out for sure anyhow.

"How's Templeton and Sara Scudder, Ben?"

He didn't know, but they turned out fine. No further arrests were ever made, and no more victims ever turned up. The missing persons reports that matched Henry's type were looked into and eventually accounted for. Dave billed Sally Scudder, not aggressively. Her money didn't look like it would hold out long, and Dave's a softy for that sort of thing. Archie Carnes, on the other hand, was absolutely animated in his congratulations and thanks to us for catching, and killing, the bad guy. It took two weeks, but I happened to open the glove box in Dave's sedan, and found a thousand dollars and a thank you note, in addition to all the car repairs that Carnes had paid for. I sent him a thank you letter back, and apologized for the delay.

If you're keeping close track, there's one loose end to tie up. It was three months later before it got done. Elsa Beltor, Henry's first helper that we saw him with, was picked up, alive and well, hitchhiking back from Montana. Goldstein had told us she was a true believer too. Not in some twisted kind of way, like Henry, but she had run off and joined a commune. After a couple months of hard work for the group, with no pay, she came back and got back in school.

FREE OFFER

Ready for more mysteries? Try any of the other David and Trait stories, available on Amazon.

Keep up with new mysteries as they're written by signing up to our monthly newsletter at www.davidandtrait.com. You'll receive two eBook shorts for your trouble.

I'm so glad to have you along.

Shane Chastain

Made in the USA
Monee, IL
06 August 2021

75116123R00111